LAND OF MANY COLORS
and
NANNA-YA

Land of
Many Colors

AND

Nanna-ya

MARYSE CONDÉ

Translated by Nicole Ball
Introduction by Leyla Ezdinli

University of Nebraska Press
Lincoln and London

This book is supported
in part by a grant from the
National Endowment for the Arts.
Pays Mêlé suivi de Nanna-ya © Editions
Robert Laffont, S.A., Paris, 1997.
Translation and introduction copyright
© 1999 by the University of Nebraska
Press. All rights reserved
Manufactured in the United States of
America. ⊚ Library of Congress
Cataloging-in-Publication Data. Condé,
Maryse. [Pays mêlé. English] Land of
many colors : and Nanna-ya / Maryse
Condé : translated by Nicole Ball;
introduction by Leyla Ezdinli.   p.   cm.
ISBN 0-8032-1488-x (cloth : alk. paper).
ISBN 0-8032-6395-3 (pbk. : alk. paper)
I. Ball, Nicole, 1941–   II. Condé, Maryse.
Nanna-ya. English. III. Title. IV. Title:
Nanna-ya. PQ3949.2.C65P3913 1999
843 – dc21   98-39182 CIP

CONTENTS

INTRODUCTION

Literary critic Françoise Pfaff beautifully underscores Maryse Condé's significance in the contemporary French and Francophone literary world in the opening of her collection of interviews with the author when she writes:

> Acclaimed in France, Africa, and the Caribbean, Maryse Condé is a novelist, playwright, essayist, and author of short stories and children's books. With her provocative characters, arresting themes, beautifully crafted language, and innovative narrative techniques, she is widely recognized as one of the most original talents to appear on the French and Francophone literary scene in recent years. Her contributions to literature won her the coveted French awards Le Grand Prix Littéraire de la Femme (1986) and Le Prix de l'Académie Française (1988). (ix)

While Maryse Condé has become recognized as an important writer in the French-speaking world, it is important to note that, through translations of her work and her activity as a scholar and teacher, she has also gained a great deal of prominence in the English-speaking world. As recent critical volumes dedicated to her work attest, Maryse Condé has proven to have a powerful voice in addressing issues of the black diaspora and of women's experiences within that diaspora.

Introduction

Maryse Boucolon was born in 1937 in Guadeloupe, a colony of France that became an overseas department after legislation passed in 1946 that gave departmental status to Martinique, Guadeloupe, Réunion Island, and French Guiana. Raised in a middle-class environment as the youngest of eight children, the author frequently refers to her childhood as a period of pampered boredom. Her mother was a schoolteacher, her father a banker. In 1953, at the age of sixteen, she left the island for Paris to study at the Lycée Fénelon and then at the University of Paris. In 1959 she married her first husband, the Guinean actor Mamadou Condé, with whom she had four children, Sylvie, Aïcha, Leïla, and Denis. She spent the next ten years primarily teaching literature in different parts of Africa, first in the Ivory Coast, then Guinea, Ghana, and finally, Senegal. She describes these years as a time of increasing political awareness during which she met militant Marxists and was able to hear revolutionary speakers such as Malcolm X, Che Guevara, and Kwame Nkrumah. Her marriage had fallen apart by 1964, although she and her husband did not officially divorce till much later, in 1981. When Kwame Nkrumah lost power in Ghana in 1966, Condé took her children and left for London, where she worked briefly for the BBC. She later moved to Senegal, where she met her second husband, Richard Philcox, in 1969. Philcox was an English teacher in the United Nations Association Program at the time and has since translated much of her work into English.

In 1970, Maryse Condé returned to Paris. There, she worked at the journal *Présence Africaine* as an author and editor while writing a thesis in comparative literature about the stereotypes of blacks in Caribbean literature. She also taught at the University of Paris X, the University of Paris VII, and the University

of Nanterre before joining the faculty of the University of Paris
IV to teach African and West Indian literature. By the time she
received her doctorate in 1975, she had published numerous
articles and two plays, *Dieu nous l'a donné* [God gave it to us]
(1972) and *Mort d'Oluwémi d'Ajumako* [Death of Oluwemi of
Ajumako] (1973). Since the early 1970s, Condé has published
prolifically in a number of genres, including critical essays, plays,
and novels. The author's path to critical prominence, however,
was not a quick one. Her first novel, *Heremakhonon* (1976), was
originally attacked by critics as politically suspect (see Vèvè Clark
interview). Interestingly, this novel has subsequently proven to
be much appreciated by critics for its complex political and
narrative perspective (see, for example, Clark; Hewitt; Lionnet;
Miller; Ngate). It was only with the publication of her best-
sellers *Segu* and *The Children of Segu*, originally published in
1984 and 1985, respectively, that Condé received sustained critical
accolades for her work in the popular press.

Condé first began teaching in the United States in the late
1970s with a visiting appointment at the University of California,
Santa Barbara. Since then she has taught at various institutions,
including the University of California, Berkeley, and the University of Virginia at Charlottesville. She currently has a position
in the French department at Columbia University. She continues
to publish novels, plays, essays, and short stories. Her work gen-
erates more and more critical attention with each passing year,
placing her among the most prominent of Caribbean writers.

LAND OF MANY COLORS AND NANNA-YA
Land of Many Colors and *Nanna-ya* are important works in the
growing corpus of Maryse Condé's fiction. Originally published
in 1985, they appear at a significant moment in Condé's career —

the moment in which she relocates her explorations of racial identity from Africa to the Caribbean. Although they have been largely overlooked by critics, these novellas represent an excellent introduction to Condé's work. Both stories reveal, in condensed form, the preoccupations that mark all of Condé's work: the search for identity in the context of the African diaspora; the political significance of history; class struggles; the effects of colonial ideology in the Caribbean; fraught relations between the sexes. *Land of Many Colors* and *Nanna-ya* also introduce a new concern in the writings of Condé: the question of independence and self-determination in the Caribbean. These two stories differ from much of her other writing in that character development is minimized in favor of a diagrammatic depiction of the interaction of Caribbean peoples. As Hal Wylie has written, "The two stories of *Pays mêlé* present a literature of genealogy in which social relations are more important than individuals; the interpretation of the past is charged with political significance. Both stories follow Caribbean families through several generations. Individuals come and go so quickly the reader may be disoriented." (679)

The problem of finding an adequate English translation of the original title, *Pays mêlé*, was a central concern in bringing this translation to completion. Maryse Condé explains in an interview with Françoise Pfaff:

> In Creole, *mwen mêlé, mwen mêlé* means "I have problems." The word *mêlé* also refers to mixed blood, to people of mixed parentage. *Pays mêlé* is a play on words and refers both to a country with problems and to a country where people are of mixed blood. (Pfaff 58)

While the original French title of this volume emphasizes the racial richness and the complexity of Caribbean culture, adjectives signifying racial mixing have largely dropped out of American usage. The literal possibilities, "Mixed Country" and "Mixed-up Country," were unsatisfactory because of their pejorative undertones and the lack of the poetic vitality of the original title.

Translator Nicole Ball's choice of a title, *Land of Many Colors*, represents an elegant solution to this difficult dilemma. The word *colors* evokes a multiplicity of racial and political identities as well as the characteristics of an intensely varied geographical landscape. Similarly, *land* avoids the potentially narrow, nationalistic connotations of the word *country* in favor of a more fluid sense of region. This volume foregrounds not only the mixing of peoples and political problems but also the mixing of the history and languages of different Caribbean territories. While Condé has admitted that the title story, *Pays mêlé*, depicts the history of Guadeloupe (Pfaff 58), because she does not name the Caribbean location where the story unfolds, and because she fictionalizes many place names in the story, she effectively creates a land that is a composite of Guadeloupe and Martinique, thereby mixing the history of these two overseas departments of France. Moreover, since *Nanna-ya* is set in Jamaica, the volume further blends together the histories of Francophone and Anglophone Caribbean islands.

Land of Many Colors

The first story of the volume opens in the Caribbean in 1984 with a double death: that of the young Antoine Suréna, a member of the island's independence movement who dies in an explosion, and that of his mother Berthe, who dies shortly after learning of the death of her only child. The narrative moves backward in time as the physician who failed to save the lives of the mother and son attempts to reconstruct their genealogy in a compensatory gesture. The tale, which takes the unnamed physician two years to piece together, is marred by many gaps that can only be filled with suppositions. The narrator constantly laments the lack of information available to him, thereby raising reader awareness of the abstract significance of his quest. These omissions point to the general historical difficulty in recovering the lives of the disenfranchised, those whose existence has been largely undocumented, those for whom official records do not exist. While this problem is not specific to Caribbean historiography, it is a crucial one for Caribbean writers who seek alternatives to the colonial record. Condé's story suggests that fiction is an important tool in the process of revising the historical record.

The narrator of *Land of Many Colors* interweaves the history of the family with the history of the city so that the city, with its racial and class conflicts as well as its segregated neighborhoods, virtually becomes another character. The physician manages to trace Berthe's family line back two generations to her grandmother, Belle, a laundress in Fort Pilote in 1896, a feat of genealogy possible largely because Belle was the lover of a powerful local black politician, Jean Hilaire Endomius, recognized as one of the founders of the Socialist Party on the island (and probably modeled on the late-nineteenth-century Guadeloupian socialist leader Hégésippe Légitimus). The narrator's story is therefore framed by a specific political trajectory: his genealogy opens against the backdrop of the introduction of socialism on the island and closes with the independence movement's adoption of violence in the fight for social justice. In between, we witness the struggles of one working-class family over four generations.

Introduction

Charting Belle's dissatisfaction with her life in Fort Pilote, the narrator follows her to South America, where her story is mapped onto another landscape of fraught race relations and family intrigue. When Belle returns to Fort Pilote fifteen years later with her daughter, Pourmera, the child's alienation in her mother's birthplace is exacerbated by the racial and ethnic conflicts that dominate the city, as well as by her mother's relative indifference and the resentment of Jean Hilaire Endomius. Fort Pilote is a city shaped by the mutual animosity of mulattoes, blacks, Syrians, and Lebanese. Pourmera's descent into madness shortly after the birth of her own daughter, Berthe, is read by the doctor who treats her not as the consequence of a broken heart but as a symptom of a diseased society. Berthe's life unfolds along with the development of new neighborhoods designed by Brazilian architects for the island's rich population. When the young Berthe is entrusted to the care of the Maheux de la Folie family, the narrator elaborates the genealogy of this white middle-class family with a colonial past whose descendants began to marry interracially when the abolition of slavery destroyed their financial and social standing. This genealogy contrasts deeply with Berthe's, although there are parallels, notably in the dissatisfaction of the women with life on the island. When Berthe moves into this economically privileged environment, the narrator introduces us to what he calls the "social geography" of the capital, Sofaya, a rich city in the north essentially populated by mulattoes whose landscape differs sharply from the commercial center of Fort Pilote, where the population is primarily black.

The family continues to follow a leftist political trajectory as the story unfolds. Berthe becomes pregnant in 1963, the year that the independence movement begins to organize sufficiently to publish its manifestos. Her child, Antoine, enters nursery school during the year Fort Pilote is hit by workers' riots. As an adult, Antoine embraces politics by joining the independence movement that seeks to end French rule and create in its place a classless, color-blind society. At this point, the struggles of the family are explicitly coded as those of the island as an emerging nation. The narrator closes his story by expressing his conviction that the independence movement will eventually succeed. The last lines of the story, "What can I tell you? He was a kid like any other . . . ," spoken by the owner of the gas station where Antoine worked, serve to normalize Antoine and the independence movement, moving the politically disempowered to the center of the political stage.

Nanna-ya

Although *Nanna-ya* is set in Jamaica, it expands on many of the themes developed in *Land of Many Colors*, notably the preoccupation with genealogy, racial strife, and class conflict. The story examines how racial and ethnic divisions from Jamaica's colonial past continue into the twentieth century. The title evokes Jamaica's colonial period, the maroon wars and the slave revolts of the eighteenth century. Condé explains in her interview with Pfaff, " 'Nanna-ya' means 'Long live Nanna' and is the beginning of a song celebrating Nanny of the Maroons. It's a very popular song in Jamaica" (Pfaff 57). Maroons were the Africans who escaped from slavery and established independent communities in the Caribbean. The relationships among the maroons, African slaves, Creole slaves, the British, and the Spanish are too complicated to detail in the space of this introduction. Briefly, however, at various moments in history, the maroons both incited slave riots against colonial powers and also signed treaties with the

British according to which they would capture and return escaped slaves.

According to political scholar Barbara Bush, Nanny was a
Jamaican Windward maroon who served as a spiritual adviser
in her maroon community:

> Nanny was an obeah woman after whom two maroon settlements
> were named. . . . At the end of the First Maroon Wars in 1739, Quao,
> the leader of the Windward maroons, unlike Cudjoe, the head of the
> Leeward group, reputedly refused to accept Governor Trelawney's
> terms of treaty on the advice of Nanny, who opposed the measure.
> Legend has it that she slew English soldiers taken captive with impunity
> and her supernatural feats are still discussed by Windward maroons.
> (69-70)

While documentation on Nanny is sparse, Bush concludes
that her role was a positive one: "The role she played was
crucial to the success of the maroons. Not only was she a
tactician and political adviser, but as a spiritual leader she
assured communal loyalty and upheld the morale of the
maroons." (70)

In a manner characteristic of much of her writing, Condé's
story undertakes a critique of identity politics. *Nanna-ya* examines how the history of animosity between the maroons and
the Creole slaves comes between two characters, Grace and her
husband, George, and how each suffers within her or his family
as a result of cultural expectations about racial identity. The
story opens with Grace recollecting memories of the mother she
feared as a child. We see that Jane, a direct descendant of Nanny,
is constantly judged by the community in relation to her legendary ancestor, a measure to which she falls short by giving birth
to an illegitimate light-skinned daughter. Grace grows up feeling

racially excluded from Moore Town and the lore of Nanny because of her skin color. As in *Land of Many Colors*, we see a daughter growing up alienated from and hating the birthplace of her mother. Grace chooses to marry instead of going to the university in order to escape her mother and the maroon community of Moore Town. The man she marries has also grown up feeling alienated within his family by virtue of being illegitimate and the darkest member of the group. Genealogy again serves a compensatory function, although, whereas in *Land of Many Colors* its purpose was positive, in *Nanna-ya* it ultimately becomes destructive. As a child, George invents a genealogy that links him to Tacky, a legendary leader of slave uprisings who was killed by a maroon. Feeling trapped by his marriage to Grace, George begins to resent his wife's ancestral ties to the maroons and offsets his rage by writing a "History of Tacky." That this history is finally stolen by the connivingly ambitious daughter of a Jamaican expatriate brings an ironic closure to George's effort to elevate his status within the community. Joyce, who comes to Jamaica seeking an understanding of her father's past, ends up profiting from her status as a light-skinned mulatta and having the manuscript published under her own name. Rather than simply typing George's manuscript, Joyce edits and revises his history of Tacky, changing the narrative voice from a pompous, digressive third person to a lively first person that allows Tacky to tell his own story. In this way, Condé's text ironically allows the island's history to be revived by contact with its own diaspora.

This novella about a mythical past that becomes an obstacle to happiness in the present thematically connects *Nanna-ya* to other works by Condé, notably her first novel, *Heremakhonon*. Commenting on *Nanna-ya*, Condé has stated:

Introduction

I mainly wanted to show how a dream can distance you from reality. The protagonist was dreaming so intently about his rebellious African ancestor who had led a slave revolt, and he was so eager to write about a mythical past, that he forgot the reality around him. In the meantime, his whole family was disintegrating: his children despised him, his children were leaving home, his wife was unhappy. Only when he was free of the mythical past did he begin to learn to live in the present. (Pfaff 57)

This blindness is one that George shares with the heroine of *Heremakhonon*, Veronica, who sets off to Africa in search of mythical ancestors and ignores the suffering of those around her because of her obsession with an imaginary past. Condé's relentless problematization of the historical record will perhaps make some readers uncomfortable; her constant references to racial and ethnic betrayals will strike some as unfortunate. Her work, however, should be read as caution against using history as "an engine of war," as George does. Condé's representation of racial history is part of a larger political agenda that insists that the political priority should be social justice for all in the present. Both *Land of Many Colors* and *Nanna-ya* suggest that nationhood for Caribbean islands, Francophone and Anglophone alike, requires reconciling ancient racial and ethnic animosities and focusing on economic stability and independence from former colonial powers.

Leyla Ezdinli

WORKS CITED

Bush, Barbara. *Slave Women in Caribbean Society 1650-1838*. Bloomington: Indiana University Press; Kingston: James Currey; and London: Heinemann, 1990.

Clark, Vèvè A. "Je me suis réconciliée avec mon île: Une interview de Maryse Condé/I Have Made Peace with My Island: An Interview with Maryse Condé." *Callaloo* 12, no. 1 (winter 1989): 86-132.

————. "Developing Diaspora Literacy: Allusion in Maryse Condé's *Hérémakhonon*." In *Out of the Kumbla: Caribbean Women and Literature*, edited by Carole Boyce Davies and Elaine Savory Fido, 303-19. Trenton NJ: Africa World Press, 1990.

Hewitt, Leah D. "Meditations of Identity through the Atlantic Triangle: Maryse Condé's *Heremakhonon*." In *Autobiographical Tightropes*. Lincoln: University of Nebraska Press, 1990.

Lionnet, Françoise. *Autobiographical Voices: Race, Gender, Self-Portraiture*. Ithaca: Cornell University Press, 1989.

Miller, Christopher. "After Negation: Africa in Two Novels by Maryse Condé." In *Postcolonial Subjects: Francophone Women Writers*, edited by Mary-Jean Grèen et al., 173-85. Minneapolis: University of Minnesota Press, 1996.

Ngate, Jonathan. "Maryse Condé and Africa: The Making of a Recalcitrant Daughter?" *A Current Bibliography on African Affairs* 19, no. 1 (1986-87): 5-20.

Pfaff, Françoise. *Conversations with Maryse Condé*. Lincoln: University of Nebraska Press, 1996.

Rea, Annabelle M. Review of *Pays mêlé*. *French Review* 60, no. 6 (May 1987): 905-6.

Wylie, Hal. "Maryse Condé. *Pays mêlé suivi de Nanna-ya*." *World Literature Today* 60, no. 4 (1986): 679.

LAND OF MANY COLORS
and
NANNA-YA

Land of Many Colors

.

To Daniel Radford

1

Why am I telling this story? I have re-created it with patient research and the power of my imagination, but it may be completely false.

I am a doctor. Head Resident at Saint Hyacinth Hospital, formerly the general hospital of Fort Pilote. Which means I've seen a lot of corpses; I've seen people dying, people condemned to die, tortured people. I'm used to seeing tragedies. So why did those two deaths upset me more than the others?

On 23 January 1984, a bomb exploded in the headquarters of the biggest national liberation movement of our country, instantly killing a young man who was there, probably manning the office at that moment. They brought me the bleeding corpse. The only thing I could do was certify the death. His name was Antoine Suréna, born 24 March 1964; he was about to turn twenty. The next day, a frail, nondescript woman in a comatose state was brought in to me. I was going to send her over to the intensive care unit when I mechanically looked at her chart: an intern had scribbled "Berthe Suréna. Born 28 December 1945 in Fort Pilote."

I questioned that intern. He didn't know anything. A male nurse gave us some information. Yes, she was the mother of the young activist. When she had learned of her son's death, she had collapsed without a sound like an exhausted beast of burden. I kept working away on that motionless body. Injections. IVs. Cardiac massage. Nothing worked.

Beyond the hospital window, petrified by the heat, Fort Pilote was holding its breath, waiting for the next terrorist attack. Suréna. It didn't ring a bell. For as a true native of Fort Pilote, I am an accomplished genealogist and know everything about the origins of anybody with a name.

Suréna? No, nothing.

I was driven by my own ignorance.

It took me two years to piece the facts together, to tie up those scattered threads. I admit I had to make things up, patch up a lot of holes. Still, I feel satisfied. I haven't betrayed Berthe and her son. Maybe they deserved some other witness . . .

At any rate, here is my story. I mean, their story.

Around 1896, in our town of Fort Pilote, a Negress nicknamed Belle caught the attention of her fellow countrymen.

Until recently, nobody spoke much about Fort Pilote. The struggle for independence raging here has brought this place out of anonymity — a place seemingly destined for the torpor and stagnation typical of a small colonial trading post. Now, not a week goes by without its name making the front page of newspapers the world over. Terrorist attacks. Explosions. Car bombs. Freedom is expensive.

Let's be honest. Fort Pilote is not a beautiful city. People who live here, even those who love it, like me, have to admit that. Except for a statue of the Discoverer that is identical to the one at Columbus Circle in New York, no public or private monument attracts one's attention, and once they have taken a stroll around the Place de la Victoire, tourists hurry on to the white, sandy beaches.

Around 1896, there were no more than twelve thousand people in Fort Pilote. It was divided into three parts. Bas du Bourg, the lower town, a collection of small houses rather similar to the huts of the former slaves who had been freed not too long before; La Folie, where the wooden houses stood, with their balconies adorned with wrought iron in the style now called "colonial"; and Le Carénage, where the warehouses and the branch offices of the Bordeaux companies were concentrated and where the lard, rice, and cane sugar were weighed.

Belle lived in Bas du Bourg. She was a laundress. As she had managed to get a lot of customers in La Folie, she scoured the town carrying either a huge bundle on her head or a wooden tray covered with a madras. She was nicknamed Belle not because of her physical charms — for she was quite plain — but as an abbreviation of her first name, Mirabelle, which her mother had heard of, God knows how, and liked for the way it sounded. Now, Belle, an unattractive woman of modest origin, came to arouse the passion of Jean Hilaire Endomius, a well-known politician historians now present as one of the founders of the Socialist Party.

Jean Hilaire was a magnificent man, a powerful speaker, a tireless pamphleteer, the editorialist of *Le Cri du Nègre*, a newspaper with a circulation of sixteen hundred.

In those days, the only way for most women to move up in society was to win the favors of a well-to-do man. They usually tried to keep him through "the pleasures of bed and table." In this way, they could get a house, a piece of land, and then give birth to children who, while illegitimate, could look down on the underprivileged masses from which they came. Belle made a clean break from this tradition. She refused to move from Bas du Bourg to La Folie as Jean Hilaire offered, refused to give up her job, refused rings, bracelets, pendants, necklaces, Caribbean baskets. Jean Hilaire insisted, his passion duly increased by each obstacle. Soon the whole town was talking of nothing but his passion and the eccentricities it was driving him to. He started to neglect his wife, the daughter of a big factory owner who represented the interests of the sugar industry on the General Council, openly preferring Belle's bed to hers.

One day, Belle disappeared. The grieving Jean Hilaire completely gave in to tafia rum—something he he'd always had an inclination for, to tell the truth. Yet that did not affect his career. Although he was always half drunk, he won a seat in the National Assembly in the elections of 1898 and, for the first time in his life, left his island for France.

We shall never know—not from her, at any rate—where Belle spent her fifteen years away from Fort Pilote. When she reappeared, she was holding by the hand a little girl of eight or nine who already looked rather grown up. As plain as her mother, but with one difference: she was very fair with reddish hair, a real *chabine*. With her curling upper lip, she didn't stand out in any way, except for her first name, which was uncommon: Pourmera. Where was it from? What was its origin? What circumstances had forced it on her mother? Belle went back to her former trade. But from then on, she no longer went around town with laundry baskets or trays. Pourmera took over.

At that time, the population of Fort Pilote was nearing twenty-five thousand. A fourth district was added to the three parts of town we have already mentioned: Morne Alizé. The whites and mulattoes had taken refuge there, fleeing the unpleasant proximity of "those educated, or rather, half-educated, blacks" who, through politics, were rapidly climbing the social ladder to catch up with them.

Jean Hilaire fell back under Belle's domination as soon as she returned. When he wasn't in Paris at the National Assembly, this man, famous in his country and in his era, divided his time between the smoke-filled halls of political rallies and the humble little house of his mistress. Sitting on her bed, in his shirtsleeves, he wrote his speeches, the most famous of which has been passed on to posterity: "Come, brothers, let us march in thick ranks to the ballot box next Sunday so that the name of Jean Hilaire Endomius, crowned with victory, may prove to all . . . etc. etc. etc."

The affair between Jean Hilaire and Belle ended only upon her death.

And yet, if someone had asked Pourmera about the years her mother had lived away from Fort Pilote, the child would certainly have provided some information. The problem is, people don't care enough about children. No one ever asks them anything, so Pourmera kept all those memories locked up in her head. Sometimes they would escape, running ahead of her through the muddy alleys of Bas du Bourg up to the lanes lined with hibiscus, poinsettias, and bloodworts that led to the villas of the comfortable middle-class people for whom her mother did laundry.

Alexandra, Belle's sister, more commonly called Sandrine, had followed a Lebanese family she worked for to Kali, a small town in South America. In two years, fever had claimed the life of the wife, and the husband had been left to fend for himself with a bunch of kids. He did what so many other men do in such a case. He settled in with the servant and gave her an ambiguous but highly coveted status. In her new affluence, Alex-andra-Sandrine did not forget Belle. As her health was delicate, more exhausted each year by her pregnancies, she thought it better to share the household responsibilities with her sister for fear that her discontented Lebanese man would take in a more vigorous companion. So she brought Belle to Kali. Belle lived with her older sister for fifteen years and helped her raise the six sons and four daughters she had borne, watching over the food and doing the laundry.

When her sister died, despite the urgings of the Lebanese, she went back to Fort Pilote; all she would accept was a few pieces of jewelry that had belonged to Sandrine as a keepsake. For a moment, she almost gave in to the family's pressure to leave Pourmera behind, as the girl's fortune would thus be assured. But then she changed her mind and took her little girl along with her.

Pourmera became acquainted with the outside world in a huge fourteen-room house; the family store took up the first floor. What did they sell? Everything: knives, sabers, cloth, pots and pans, locks, animal feed. Pourmera took her first steps on the balcony overhanging a lively street filled with the din of the few cars owned by rich city folks, the donkeys of the peasant women who came to sell their vegetables, and the horses of the landowners. Like all the children of the household, she called the Lebanese man "Papa." Sandrine was "Mama" and her own mother, "Belle." She spoke Arabic and Creole before she could express herself in French (and then with difficulty), and she would cross herself in front of every image of Jesus, the Virgin Mary, and the saints. When her mother decided to leave Kali, her whole world collapsed. She never forgave her for having brought her back and conceived a childish hatred for Fort

Pilote—a blind, unfair, unrestrained hatred. Was Kali a more beautiful city than Fort Pilote? There is no reason to think so.

In 1536, a Spaniard by the name of Pedro Mendoza founded a tiny village at the edge of the waters not far from the estuary of the Rio Chico. From 1851 on, the coolie trade brought in two hundred and sixty thousand Asians, most of them Hindus.

Did they name the city after one of their deities? Present-day historians have no opinion on the matter. At any rate, when Pourmera reminisced about Kali, she saw a beautiful, carefree place, a kind of paradise meant for happiness.

In all truth, it must be said that Jean Hilaire Endomius did nothing to help Pourmera become accustomed to Fort Pilote. On the contrary, in his eyes that child was the living proof of how little he counted in Belle's life, the sign of his nothingness, of his utter harmlessness. Another man had possessed his mistress, and not surreptitiously in an ephemeral blaze of the senses; another man had gotten her pregnant in the full view of a neighborhood, of a city, of the whole world. Another man had offered her what neither gold nor diamonds can buy and had forged that indestructible bond: a child! That was why, whenever his eyes fell on Pourmera, they would fill with tears of pain and anger and he would bite his lips so as not to curse.

Getting her into a school would have been easy for him, but he enjoyed watching her grow up ignorant and uncouth, heading for a future of mediocrity and subjection.

In this drama of three characters, which did not go unnoticed, all the people who hated Jean Hilaire took Pourmera's side. And indeed there were many of them in Fort Pilote. First, the mulattoes, who could never stomach the social and political rise of that "man with next to no education, no real intelligence, but active, bustling, never one to shrink from any means of propaganda . . ." as the editorialist of *La Vérité* put it. Then there were the Negroes, who, from the beginning of time, have always hated it when one of their own rises above the others. Finally there were the Syrians and the Lebanese, who feared for their commercial interests since Jean Hilaire called them "foreign sharks." Pourmera became the child of all these people. In all the houses where she picked up or delivered laundry, there was a treat waiting for her. In the morning, a bowl of cool milk flavored with cinnamon. At lunchtime, a bit of braised fresh tuna and white rice in a *coui,* half a hollowed gourd. At snack time, coconut sherbet. In the evening, a bowl of good beef broth with a marrow bone in it. They forgave her silent ways, her strange moods, her aloofness, her purposeless wanderings. They agreed that she was slightly deranged, a bit "nutty," but that made her still more endearing to everyone.

Just when Pourmera was about to turn seventeen, Belle died.

Belle was an enigma to her fellow countrymen. In those days, when women never questioned their dependency on men or their subjection to their children, her whole behavior was shocking. We have already described how she treated Jean Hilaire Endomius. As for her only daughter, instead of cherishing her like the apple of her eye, she let her go barefoot, her heels scratched by the stones on the streets, clad in a cheap, faded cotton dress, her mop of hair reddened by sun and sweat. Actually, however harshly people judged her, she judged herself more harshly still. But no one knew that.

She had never loved Jean Hilaire, although she was sometimes flattered to have such a man in her power. Besides, Jean Hilaire bragged, not entirely without reason, that he could satisfy five women and a mare in one night, and she felt real pleasure in his arms. At the same time, as surprising as this may seem for a woman from her background, she had dreams of some other encounter, of a love that would set her ablaze and reduce her to ashes burning in a crematorium. Ah, to leave Fort Pilote, with its limited horizon! Those petty, scandal-mongering people with no ideals! A land devoid of great men or great victories! She had answered Sandrine's call in this "romantic" state of mind. As she was walking down the gangway of the boat with her basket on her head, the love she dreamed of took the shape of the Lebanese man: the very companion of her own sister.

It is a delight for a man to possess two sisters—the most complete and exquisite form of polygamy. At the same time, the Lebanese was a good Christian and his conscience tormented him. He tried to end his liaison with Belle by literally giving her to his storekeeper, Carlos Martinez, a half-breed from Bogota with sad eyes.

Despite this, clearly, his relations with Belle did not slack off. What did Sandrine think? The little testimony we have on the matter concurs: she suffered terribly. In the room where she spent more and more time because of her weakened condition, she brought in all kinds of sorcerers, those who speak to the night, those who tame its shadows and raise the waters of the sea, so that they would rid her of this rival who was also her sister. She made two pilgrimages to Sainte-Marie-des-Bons-Vents in an oxcart and poured ewe's milk, blood, and fruit pulp into the sea. All to no avail. As for Carlos Martinez, the half-breed from Bogota, no doubt weary of sharing her, he left for another coastal city in the south one fine morning, unhesitatingly abandoning his mistress and the newborn baby who, by pure chance, was his: Pourmera.

All of this ended in Sandrine's death, as we already know.

Incompetent doctors delivered permission for burial without ever finding out that she had been murdered. Not with daggers or poisons. With more secret and deadly weapons. Did Belle decide to go back to Fort Pilote because she was struck by remorse? Not at all. Although nearing fifty, the Lebanese man was still quite a handsome man, with a strapping torso, a flat belly, and legs like columns of a Greek temple. With all the passion of a middle-aged man, he had fallen for an Italian girl, a daughter of those immigrants who came by the millions between 1850 and the First World War "to build America," and he intended to marry her in church "in a veil and bridal wreath." Belle couldn't stand that idea, despite his assurances that he would never part from her. Did she have something else in mind? Had she dreamed of moving into the large second-floor bedroom where her sister, despite her humiliation, had slept as mistress of the house, facing reproductions of painted Portuguese tile and a tortured Christ sculpted by Aleijadinho . . . ? There is absolutely no proof of that.

The fact is, she cleared out, bag and baggage, and went back to Fort Pilote. Like her daughter, but for different reasons, she hated the town. She had thought she'd left it for good. It seemed to her that nothing had changed in fifteen years: lined with latania palms, the river that cut Fort Pilote in two still carried along in its muddy waters the pettiness, the nastiness, the narrow vision and ambitions of a small colonial society. So we're not surprised by her increased detachment from Jean Hilaire, nor by her indifference to her daughter.

That woman lived elsewhere. She had remained in Kali and poeticized it, transforming into broad avenues its badly tarred streets, flooded at the first rains; into palaces its low houses forming "barrios" — an expression borrowed from the neighboring Spanish-speaking country—with their bougainvilleas, cannas, tulip trees, and of course, their hibiscus; into vast parade grounds its small, triangular public square in the center of town where slaves were whipped in the old days and where women now sold fritters of manioc, dried shrimp, coconut, or cashew. What was happening to the Lebanese man? How many children had he fathered on his new bride—all-white children destined to lord it over their mulatto brothers? Belle would choke and squeeze her lips tight so as not to scream with pain.

2

The day after her mother died, when she had been buried under the Indian almond trees of the Briscaye graveyard that looks out on the sea, Pourmera changed. The young woman everyone had thought nutty, slow, or at any rate incompetent went to the Sisters of Christian Instruction and knocked at their door. The mother superior's welcome lacked enthusiasm, but could she really turn down a sheep that had lost its shepherd? To cover the cost of board and tuition, Pourmera was assigned to work at the laundry and linen room, where she turned out to have a magic touch. Delicate mending, embroidering, crochet lacing, smocking, gathering — she was a success at everything she did. Three years later, she could read, write, and count. So she left the Sisters and opened up a novelty shop she named The Silver Thimble. Where did she find the money to set up her own business? Certain documents permit me to assert that she turned to her adoptive father, the Lebanese, who quickly transferred a significant sum of money via the Bank of Paris and the Netherlands and had fancy goods from Paris sent to her.

In a few years, Pourmera became almost a lady.

We must recall that in those days, social categories were not clearly defined; as the whole society was still close to the mold of slavery, people admired ingenuity, resourcefulness, and an enterprising spirit. So and so, born to an unknown father and a servant mother, became the owner of a construction business. So and so, the illegitimate son of a lowly town hall clerk, became a printer and made lawyers out of his sons. Of course girls had a harder time climbing the social ladder, so Pourmera's success was even more admirable.

It is now 1930. Fort Pilote has a population of 28,604.

The wholesale business has spread out its warehouses and occupies the whole district of docks bordering the harbor. The novelty business — cloth, garments, fashion, furniture, household utensils — has thrived, and as a result, neighborhoods have become more lively; small or retail businesses have improved, sprouted, organized into guilds. Or so historians say.

But let us return to Pourmera. She was living in quite a nice house in La Folie, not very big, four or five rooms, an attic, running water, electricity, and a shower in the courtyard. She had her own pew on a side aisle of the cathedral of Saint-Benoît. She even hired a little maid who shopped for her and vigorously splashed down her portion of sidewalk. There was only one dark spot on this picture of well-being: Pourmera lived alone. No one had ever seen her with a male friend or a lover. No companion in her bed. People whispered among themselves that this was not healthy. Women were meant to receive seed. Women were meant to bear children.

Now at this point, some kind of red-headed Negro no one had ever heard of showed up in town.

His name was Abelardo, which makes us think he was of Spanish descent. Yet he spoke perfect Creole and his French was quite good. Maybe he simply was a Negro from the French Caribbean who had lived in Latin America.

Anything is possible. He got himself hired in one of the stores of the Carénage district, first as an errand boy, then as a stock-keeper. How did he manage to meet Pourmera, who, we may recall, was then going on forty? But love can strike anywhere, a well-known fact, and so Pourmera and Abelardo's affair shouldn't come as a surprise. Nevertheless, if the people of Fort Pilote were convinced of the intensity of Pourmera's love, they unanimously doubted Abelardo's feelings for her. They saw how he had settled into the house in La Folie; they could see how he was now sitting behind the cash register of The Silver Thimble, how he gave orders to the maid. He was never seen at the cathedral, though, for he was an unbeliever, a jolly drinker, and he greatly enjoyed cursing of the worst kind.

I must cut short this part of my story, which is far too predictable. Abelardo revealed his true nature.

In a few years, he dragged Pourmera into total ruin. Harassed by creditors, she had to sell her store and her house, including all of its contents. This is how her heavy oak furniture happened to fall into the hands of one of Jean Hilaire Endomius's legitimate daughters, who, because she hated Belle and her offspring as much as her mother had before her, saw in this the vengeance of God. At this point, Abelardo disappeared and went off to spread grief to other parts of the world. Pourmera was left all alone. Soon afterwards, she realized she was pregnant. Is maternal love a complete invention? Perhaps the question should be debated. The generations of women who have abandoned their children in the gutter or on garbage dumps might confirm this thesis. On the other hand, all the women who are staunch supporters of the joys of motherhood might refute it. In Pourmera's case, there is absolutely no doubt about it: she felt no love for the seven-pound little girl she gave birth to on a December evening who was given the name of Berthe. We have just said that Pourmera felt no love for her baby. This is not exactly true. She simply was not interested. Whenever the nurses put the little creature in her arms, she wouldn't look at her and would hold her so loosely that she could have dropped her. She refused to nurse. Besides, they soon realized she had no milk and the child would only have sucked on an empty calabash. Mother and daughter stayed in the hospital for quite some time, for they had to perform a caesarian operation on Pourmera, who was too old and had taken no part in her own delivery. When she recovered, since they had nowhere to go, a woman named Black-Eyed Martha talked her husband Marcius into taking in the mother and child. Black-Eyed Martha had worked with Pourmera at the Sisters of Christian Instruction as a helper in the laundry room, and in her brief period of prosperity, Pourmera had never forgotten her.

It was a few weeks after the baby's birth that Pourmera started to howl at night.

The first time it happened, Black-Eyed Martha thought it was a stray dog conversing with death. She was about to step outside to throw a bucket of cold water at it when she realized her mistake. She ran into the next room and found Pourmera completely naked, her frail body drenched in sweat, arched like a bow. She was throwing her head out backward and from her rather short, shapely lips that disclosed her extremely white and pointy teeth a horrible cry was spurting out. Thank God, the baby was sound asleep in her cradle. Black-Eyed Martha, at a loss about what to do, woke up Marcius, who ran out to get a neighbor; they got her to swallow lots of asafetida, rubbed her vigorously with turpentine and volatile alkali, and somehow managed to calm Pourmera down. The same thing happened again the next day and every single night thereafter. It was like a well-oiled machine. At 11:30 P.M. sharp, Pourmera would start raising hell. It lasted, with some moments of respite, until about 3:00 A.M.

After three months of this, Black-Eyed Martha and Marcius resigned themselves to consulting Doctor Blonfort. Doctor Blonfort was the son of Isaac Blonfort, who had been elected senator in 1885, reelected in 1894, and was one of the founders of the League for the Defense of the Rights of Man and the Citizen. This entitled him to be part of the Fort Pilote elite, but he remained very simple and generous, often treating people at no charge. When Pourmera was brought to him, he confessed that he was utterly unable to help. He consulted a French doctor who had no clue either. After much hesitation, they decided to commit Pourmera to the Baumettes Hospital on 28 September 1947. Her daughter was about to turn two.

The way they treated mentally ill patients at the Baumettes Hospital of Fort Pilote had certainly improved. Patients were no longer chained and their clothes tied with ropes. In short, people thought mad were no longer punished for what was still considered their own fault. Work was the main way of managing the guilty patient. They made sure they kept the insane women active, and so, very appropriately, Pourmera was given clothes to mend and especially to embroider. When evening came, she got heavy doses of what would later be called tranquilizers so that she would not disturb her fellow inmates' sleep. On the other hand, she was well fed.

Pourmera's illness and then her hospitalization caused a sensation in Fort Pilote. It was as if she was again becoming the child she once was, an object of pity and affection, a victim, a scapegoat whose sufferings filled the hardest of hearts with rage. Some talked about tracking Abelardo down and prosecuting him. But what would he be accused of? Ruining a woman's life? If this was a crime punishable by law, a lot of men would find themselves behind bars. A young lawyer by the name of Michel Desnard did some research along these lines but he soon gave up.

What did Pourmera think of, dressed in her gray hospital gown, her hair tied in four buns, her eyes lost in space? We have no way of knowing. Was she remembering Kali, the house she was born in, the face of her father, Carlos Martinez, who'd leave home for days at a time, her aunt Sandrine, who had been a victim just as she was, her uncle Lucien, and all the children he had fathered — white, brown, chocolate, caramel-colored? Or rather, was she thinking of her mother? She had hated her for not having loved her, for not having cared for her as mothers should. Yet here she was, following in her mother's footsteps, abandoning her daughter to the care of strangers, a lonely child, forever stigmatized. At this time in her life, she understood Belle. She came to realize that in the wreckage of love and hopes, a child does not count. She blamed herself for not having been close to her, to console her and open her heart. Paradoxically, she did not give much thought to Berthe, a small bundle of wrinkled flesh, a sickly excrescence of her love.

But mostly, her thoughts must have turned to Abelardo. What was happening to him? How many children had he produced with other women, naive and gullible like herself? How many bank accounts had shrunk because of his extravagance? Yet she held no grudge against him. Imprisoned in her calico smock, her now-despised body remembered, and she would press her lips together so as not to howl again, because if she did, the male nurse would come up to her and urge her not to disturb the peace of the community. And she couldn't stand the way he spoke to her.

The search Michel Desnard had conducted to track Abelardo down had not been a very careful one. If he had done a better job, he would have found him a few islands farther on, in the little town of Sangre Grande. Abelardo had rented a room in a grim hotel located in a working-class neighborhood full of shacks; this hotel had a mezzanine and was not too far from the painted wood villas surrounded by groves of eucalyptus and mango trees where rich people once lived. At the time Pourmera was committed, the rainy season was on. The streets of Sangre Grande had turned into muddy streams that had to be forded on big stones placed at regular intervals. With Pourmera's money, Abelardo had bought shares in a Caribbean shipping company that was supposed to provide service to all the islands of the archipelago and to some countries in Central America, an unrealizable project, like all the others he had been involved in. The company offices were to occupy the fifth floor of the only skyscraper, still under construction, the Soroboca Building, but the treasurer as well as the general director of the company were a long time coming.

Abelardo would often think of Pourmera. Not that he loved her. He felt for her the kind of pity somewhat similar to the tenderness men feel for the women they have used and abused. But I can't be too hard on him. He knew nothing of her pregnancy nor of the birth of Berthe. If he had heard about it, his behavior might have been different. He would have liked to write her but he didn't know how to start his letter. At the same time, his boredom lent a poetic quality to Fort Pilote and he would forget how he had mocked its people and their ways. If

22

his shipping company project fell through, he wasn't sure what he would do. Go back to the casa hacienda and load his shoulders with bales of cotton? He would rather die.

And yet, the kind of death he rejected with all his thoughts came to meet Abelardo. Completely by chance. You have to realize that on this island, plantation workers were subjected to a type of sharecropping system called *compagnonnage* that bound them, most often verbally, to landlords by means of a one-year contract. Now, at the end of the Second World War, the time our story takes place, this system no longer seemed profitable. The big landlords were starting to take complete charge of their land and create companies they incorporated in order to facilitate their shift to capitalism. The *compagnonnage* system was being dismantled. Bands of farmers were now flocking into the towns, getting drunk on their last pennies and getting into fights with their machetes, which had become useless in the urban jungles. Perhaps what these men lacked were leaders who could turn their anger and frustration into revolutionary rage! Without such leaders, many brawls and short-lived riots spilled blood into one downtown slum or another.

And so one night in a dirty, smoky bar, Abelardo was gulping down a few glasses of *pinga*, a drink made from sugarcane, but very different from rum, mixed with iced lemon juice. He knew that when the mountain ridge stood out like a hard, jagged leaf against the slightly clearer sky, he would be happily drunk. He would forget that he had once more gotten into a dead end and that he would soon find himself with his back to the wall. We don't know for sure why a fight broke out at the other end of the bar. The fact is that Abelardo interfered and was knifed a few times. He lost a lot of blood and thus, a little later, also lost his life at Sisters of the Visitation Hospital. A death without glory.

People with inventive minds will enjoy making conjectures. What would have happened if Abelardo had not died that day? Back against the wall, penniless, would he have gone back to Pourmera? Would this have cured her madness, since, in actual fact, all she was doing was waiting for him? Would he have held his child in his arms? Would he have loved her? Could he have made her mother love her? And if he did, would Berthe's life have been different? Wondering in this way is pointless, as the reality is what has just been recorded. No one knows where Abelardo's grave is and no one cares.

3

So Berthe was born on 28 December 1945. Berthe was the name of the midwife who attempted to deliver the baby before calling the doctor. As Pourmera was incapable of choosing a first name from the list of saints' names on the calendar, she was faced with making the decision all by herself. The child was officially given the family name Suréna, which, before her, had been her mother's and grandmother's name. Berthe Suréna.

Despite the circumstances surrounding her birth — of which she obviously knew nothing — Berthe was a happy little girl up to the age of five. As far as she was concerned, her mummy was Black-Eyed Martha and her daddy was Marcius, a carpenter. She grew up in the small garden next to the little house, among the convolvulus and the roses, learning not to uproot ironweeds, lemon balm, and crabgrass because Black-Eyed Martha used them to make herb tea. When she was tired of playing she would go into Marcius's workshop and wrap shavings of wood around her fingers, breathing in the smell of turpentine and varnish. She had inherited the fragility of her mother and grandmother but her face was more attractive, for Abelardo's beautiful slanted eyes made up for Pourmera's very flat nose and overly short mouth and composed a lovely, touching little face. When she turned six, she entered school.

I don't know if she was taught the famous sentence that begins "Our ancestors the Gauls had blue eyes . . ." that present generations here are now rebelling against, but I am certain that they made a circle around her, chanting in a singsong: "Your mother is crazy, she's in the nuthouse, nya-nya-nya poo poo . . ."

Berthe had absolutely no idea what these words meant. She could only tell they meant being excluded. She ran back home under the warm late-morning sun, through the alleys of what had become the "old town," which now included the La Folie and Bas du Bourg districts put together, as opposed to the Morne Alizé and Morne Moustique areas, late offshoots of the new neighborhoods where the nouveaux riches lived in their new villas designed by Brazilian architects. All out of breath, she repeated to Black-Eyed Martha and Marcius what she had just heard. They were taken aback. The following Sunday, after they had discussed the matter endlessly with Doctor Blonfort, they took Berthe to the Baumettes Hospital.

As we have said, the Baumettes Hospital was neither a forced labor camp nor a place where people were tortured. It was a five-story structure of a dirty white color with a bare, severe front except for a niche located at the level of the third floor, inside of which stood the full-length statue of Francis Orlando des Baumettes; he had been governor of the island and had built the hospital in 1802 in remembrance of his mother, who had died insane a few years before. In the back, the hospital opened onto a huge park divided in two by a now-defunct railroad that had been used for the transportation of sugarcane. The lower part was planted with icacoes, their flesh pink as children's wounds, and guava trees.

Were there ever any patients who left the Baumettes Hospital for good? We must admit that it was not common. This occurrence has only been recorded three times in ten years, and more-over, it seems that the people who did leave were not really mentally ill but had families who wanted to get rid of them. At the time Berthe came to visit her, Pourmera was a little past fifty. She seemed like a child who had leaped directly into old age. Her white hair was carefully greased with carapa oil. Her ears and neck had been rubbed with bay rum so they would smell nice, and she was sitting, slightly hunched up, in a high-backed chair.

"Give your mom a kiss . . ."

Berthe obediently put her fresh mouth on the tepid, wrinkled cheek, soft as blotting paper. All those watching the scene— Doctor Blonfort, Black-Eyed Martha, Marcius, two nurses— waited for some sign, some trigger, a miraculous cure as in Lourdes, when the cripples throw away their pallets and start to walk. Nothing happened. The slanting eyes showed nothing. The lips did not grimace upwards to form an expression that could have passed for a smile. In the general silence, a nurse offered Berthe an apple from France, bright red, all shiny as if polished. The child dug her teeth into it as Doctor Blonfort was stroking her cheek. The visit did not last very long, for it was September, right in the middle of the rainy season. Around six in the evening, the rain would start and pierce the tin roofs with its sharp needles.

The following morning, Berthe could not get up. She com-plained of heaviness in her head.

The thermometer read one hundred and three. In the after-noon, she went into convulsions. Doctor Blonfort, who had been called in right away, admitted to having been wrong to authorize the meeting and forbade that the child should ever see her mother again. Once the fever was gone, Berthe fell into an agitated state of muteness, with eyes closed and eyelids quivering; Doctor Blonfort was anxiously watching over that agitated muteness. Holding the small hand in his big hand and squeezing it, he would have liked to read the little girl's mind. What kind of thoughts and images were jostling about in her brain? He felt overwhelmed with remorse. He had only prescribed what he thought right, for he belonged to a school of psychiatrists who met once a year and had just held a conference in Philadelphia. That school loudly claimed that madness was produced by the destruction society imposes on mentally ill patients and the destruction they impose on themselves; madness was a disguise, a pretense, a grotesque caricature.

That school of psychiatry was of the opinion that mad people should be returned to their family, to life, as in those African villages where the mentally ill walk about freely and mingle with sane men and women. Were they wrong?

Berthe seemed to recover from the confrontation with her mother. She went back to playing, running, eating *kilibibi* or *kakodou* candies. Maybe the children at school did torment her again but she learned how to defend herself and she never said another word about it to Black-Eyed Martha or Marcius.

Miss Latéral, a teacher she had in those years, has practically no memory of her student. She obviously was not one of the little girls with light skin and a well-to-do family she made sure she called on every day. Neither was she one of the dummies whose stupidity remains indelibly engraved in a teacher's mind. She was a gentle, rather quiet little girl whose notebooks were kept relatively neatly, who recited La Fontaine's fable "The Fox and the Crow" expressively enough, and who went completely unnoticed.

And then, Black-Eyed Martha's older brother happened to die. At the age of seventeen, he had moved to a Spanish-speaking island — Canete — where he had started a small coffee company that by now was thriving. As he had neither wife nor children, this asset reverted in its entirety to Black-Eyed Martha. Who has never harbored the dream of becoming the owner of a successful business? Black-Eyed Martha and Marcius made up their minds right away. The carpentry shop brought in nothing, so they decided to sell their meager possessions and emigrate to Canete. There was only one dark spot on the picture: Berthe. What would they do with that little girl, nearly ten years old, whose schooling was all French and who was used to living in a specific environment? Could they transplant her into a totally different country on an isolated estate thirty-five hundred feet high, far from any other town? Again, they had an endless discussion with Doctor Blonfort. He was the one who found the family they could entrust Berthe to, the Aubrun family, to whom he was related on the women's side.

To understand fully the nature of the family that agreed to take care of Berthe, it may be useful to go far back before the time in which our story takes place.

Around 1860, the Maheux de la Folie, a *béké* family, white French Creoles, ruined by the abolition of slavery and the ensuing social turmoil, made a decision of the utmost importance. They decided to marry their children to mulattoes. This should not be taken as a sign of broad-minded opinions and a healthy lack of prejudice. Their plan was a clever one. Jos Maheux de la Folie, head of the clan, understood that mulattoes were now the new ruling class. Weren't they buying back the rum distilleries, the coffee and cacao plantations? The Belle-Eau plantation had just fallen into their hands. How many acres of good farmland did they own already? How many more acres would they soon have? He had to hurry before the mulattoes had everything they wanted and became arrogant and uncompromising. The ones from the Sofaya area rushed to get the Maheux de la Folie girls, delightfully blond, deliciously beautiful, who could all sing Schubert lieder so ravishingly. The Maheux de la Folie boys did not pick wives beyond a certain skin color and bank account. After much hesitation, Charles Emmanuel, Jos's elder son, resolved to ask for Emma Devarieux's hand. They had a very happy marriage. They had ten children: five boys, five girls. At a very early age, Belia, the youngest, turned out to be a child prodigy.

Around 1896, at the time Belle attracted the attention of her fellow countrymen in Fort Pilote, seventy-five miles away from Sofaya, Belia published a novel called *Under the Caribbean Sun*. Opinions about titles for novels have changed. Today, we would probably find this one a bit tacky, overloaded with exoticism even to the point of being "doudouist." But at the time, such a title was aggressive and provocative. It was a good reflection of Belia's intentions: she wanted to expose all the sordid deals, self-centered calculations, and hypocrisy of the society she belonged to. *Under the Caribbean Sun* shocked the public. Now it seems unreadable, for our conception of writing has also changed. The irritating Petrarchan dialogues between lovers and certain incongruous melodramatic effects would make the reader smile. Jos Maheux de la Folie nearly had a heart attack when he read the book, and rumor has it that the portrait his granddaughter made of him hastened his death.

Then Belia decided that the island was too small to harbor her genius, and she left the very same year Belle sailed to Kali in order to help Sandrine. What countries did she go to? First, to France. Her presence is reported in Parisian literary circles. At which point, we somehow lose track of her, only to find her again, years later, on Largo do Boticario in Rio de Janeiro. She lived in a house that had a light blue front with four high windows; two of them had an iron-railed balcony crowded with plants. You entered through a large studded door into a cool patio. For let us not forget that Belia never really wanted for money. As her father's favorite daughter, all she had to do was give a call for help and he would immediately comply. The start of her moral downfall seems to come after Rio, when she was abandoned by the man she loved.

For the next fifteen years she wandered around. She finally came back to Sofaya, her hair prematurely white and pretty much an alcoholic, as the family soon realized to their horror, with a shy, beautiful child who could not speak a word of French clinging to her skirts. The name of that child was Altagras. There's no point going on about her childhood and adolescence. To say they were not happy is enough. Among circles that think of themselves as aristocratic, no compassion is wasted on stray lambs. Belia was branded, and her bastard daughter, whose father was a matter of speculation for the whole region, was also despised, excluded, excommunicated. To escape from her hellish life, at the age of twenty she entered into a loveless marriage with a Negro veterinarian — Emmanuel, known as Mano, Aubrun. She had three children by him: two sons, Antoine and Jean-François, and a daughter, Dominique.

These were the people Berthe was to live with. Theoretically, Doctor Blonfort's plan had been fairly sensible. He absolutely wanted to place Berthe in a middle-class family who would care about bringing her up properly and giving her a good education, but one that wasn't too rich or proud and would thus not be tempted to treat her like a servant. Moreover, his mother was a second cousin of Mano Aubrun, a man who liked him and whom he himself respected.

In practice, the good doctor's choice proved to be a disaster; so his decisions twice had a negative effect on the course of Berthe's life and on her personality. In those days, women were not sufficiently consulted; this cannot be overemphasized. If Doctor Blonfort had dealt with Altagras Aubrun, everything would have been different. But he merely had a talk with Mano, who was very busy, paid little attention, and above all, did not want to give the impression that he was not master in his own house.

When Berthe started to share her life, Altagras Aubrun was, at forty, a very beautiful woman. A mulatta whose black blood shone through gloriously. Her skin the color of honey, her ebony hair finely grooved as if with an iron tool, her mouth fleshy with slightly purple contours, and a sensual expression she could not hide despite her religious devotions. All the young males of the middle class, familiar with the many residences of the Maheux de la Folie clan, had dreamed of holding her in their arms. And yet none of them had asked for her hand; holding a bouquet of white flowers between her fingers, she had seen her cousins getting married one after the other. Even the shy and sickly Germaine. So she caught on and accepted the Negro Mano Aubrun.

How awful for a woman to have to share her bed with a man she does not love! To suffer his embrace night after night and even during the hot afternoons when the whole house is asleep. Unfortunately for Altagras, Mano was like Jean Hilaire Endomius: they were the type of men who boast they can satisfy in a few hours five women and a mare. Several times a day she had to suffer that weight, receive into her the brutal member that pulled pleasure out of her against her will, and submit to touchings in the most secret parts of her body. Helpless and desperate, she would start to imagine the worst: Mano's Citroën hit a palm tree on Dumanoir Drive; the horse Mano was riding as he went down to the valleys to attend to the farmers' cattle had bolted and dragged his body for miles on a trail full of volcanic rocks. As she reached in her dreams the exact moment when she was bending down to verify his death, a hard hand would take her by the shoulder and a passionate voice would whisper:

"Come on, honey, give it to me . . . !"

Mano's words were even more repulsive to her than the act following them.

Why is it that Altagras did not love Mano, a man so many heiresses of the best families around had longed for, including Jean Hilaire Endomius's legitimate daughters? It would be simplistic to attribute such a feeling to contempt for her husband's color. Rather, we believe that this intelligent, proud woman hated the subservient condition marriage put her in, the impossibility for her sex to choose its destiny, to make mistakes or to accomplish things that make life worthwhile. Belia, her mother, had paid too high a price for her freedom. She did not have the strength to imitate her and she was consumed by her lack of courage. Rocking back and forth on her veranda, she pictured herself in Paris, Madrid, Rio de Janeiro, the places where her mother had lived. People would whisper:

"She's Altagras Maheux de la Folie. The author of . . ."

For she had written a novel, far superior to *Under the Caribbean Sun*, a novel for which she had won a famous literary prize. Then she would open her eyes and be back on the Rue du Sable

again, a street abutting the sea on one side, the foothills of the
Morne à Vaches on the other. At the crossroad, the snowball
vendor would shake his little bell. Mademoiselle Destremaux
was heading toward the cathedral to attend Vespers . . .

Luckily, Altagras had her eldest son, Antoine, to comfort her.
The youngest ones didn't count, as if she had exhausted with
him, all at once, the treasures of her heart. Antoine was a true
Maheux de la Folie, the spitting image of Charles Emmanuel,
his maternal grandfather.

Until he reached the age of five, Altagras's happiness was
perfect. She dressed him in sailor suits, rolled his long silky hair
into ringlets, touched the back of his neck with her perfumed
finger and took him to church for everyone to admire. Unfortunately, at that age he was struck with convulsive meningitis, and
although he survived, he remained retarded for the rest of his
life. He practically lost the use of speech and had to leave school.
Sometimes he would urinate on himself.

Everybody who knew her agrees that from then on, Altagras's
personality, which was already difficult, changed completely.
She became bitter, sarcastic, avoided people even more than she
had before, and no longer left her home on the Rue du Sable
except to go to mass. Nobody dared ask her about her son's
condition, for she would violently rebuff them. Moreover, as
time went on, she stopped saying hello to people.

As for her husband, Mano Aubrun, he took his son's sickness
in stride.

Mano Aubrun had been tempted by politics because, as we
said before, it was the best way for Negroes to rise in society,
along with education. Yet, at the time he was coming of age, in
the thirties that is, things were not that simple anymore. Half a
century earlier, all it had taken to create a newspaper and found

the Socialist Party was a small group of former students from the lycée of Fort Pilote, all of modest background. For these young men, what was at stake was clear. In the society following the abolition of slavery, even though all citizens were declared equal, the color black remained a handicap. Socialism, an egalitarian ideology, the daughter of great republican principles, seemed to provide an answer to that contradiction. At present, society had already been stratified into classes and the established black bourgeoisie was just as arrogant as the middle class of the mulattoes. Mano was not really born into its center; rather, he was at the edge, even if his father was an honorable school teacher. Breaking through required energy and talent; he had neither and merely made do with his profession. He was among the first to study in France, but as he lived in Bordeaux, he found himself left out of the intellectual excitement of his fellow citizens studying in Paris. That is how he never heard about Negritude and was never involved in the budding struggle against colonialism.

4

I have not forgotten Berthe. She is almost ten. She is on the docks, holding Doctor Blonfort's hand and watching the *Dona Flor* carrying Black-Eyed Martha and Marcius away to the island of Canete.

"Don't cry," she was told. "You'll see them again during summer vacation . . ."

So she tries not to cry. The day before, a certain Doctor Emmanuel Aubrun came to see Black-Eyed Martha and Marcius and assured them that their little girl would be fine in his home. As with most children, curiosity — about this new life opening up in front of her — triumphs over apprehension. And the doctor looks like a nice man, too. Now Doctor Blonfort leads her to his car, an American car, a Studebaker. She has never been in such a beautiful car.

The Aubruns lived on the Rue du Sable in Fort Pilote. At this point, it may be useful to provide some information about the social geography of the island. The northern part, mountainous and planted with trees, has traditionally been occupied by the mulattoes after the *békés* were forced to leave the economic scene; whereas the southern part, flat and often swampy, has been settled by the Negroes on pieces of land sometimes no larger than half an acre. Two towns display this bipolarisation.

36

To the north, Sofaya, the capital, essentially inhabited by mulattoes, founded in 1640 deep inside a magnificent bay, although its open harbor is somewhat shallow. To the south, Fort Pilote, a commercial center with a motley but predominantly black population. The Maheux de la Folies had their fief above Sofaya, in the Carmel region, and scorned everyone who lived below a line going from Anse Paradis to Camarene, twenty miles beyond Sofaya. Of course, in the fifties, all these distinctions were not so strict anymore: an unpredictable bureaucracy, the job market, and the growth of tourism had led to a great deal of mobility. But for Altagras, "going down" from Sofaya to settle in Fort Pilote with her husband was the very symbol of her downfall. And yet, the house on the Rue du Sable was such a beautiful house, under its roof of red tiles with their patina of age, its bare white front with no balcony, lit at night by a hexagonal lantern. It had ten rooms and an attic.

When Berthe arrived at the Aubruns, the family was about to have dinner. The table was set, and on each plate there was a cloth napkin case with its owner's name—Papa, Mama, Antoine, Dominique, Jean-François—embroidered on it in stem stitch, and for Berthe, this seemed to symbolize her new life. Then all the participants came in and took their seats. Strangely enough, though, Altagras did not seem to make a strong impression on Berthe that evening. She may have frightened her a little, but no more than any other adult would have. Altagras was holding a little girl by the hand. A very small boy was squirming in his father's arms. At one point, Altagras ordered a servant who was sticking an inquisitive head through the curtains to take Berthe to her room on the third floor. And there, sitting on the highest step, his face against the railing, was this little boy who was watching the visitors but did not want to be seen.

Berthe was a rather shy girl. But she found somewhere inside herself the courage to ask:

"What's your name?"

The servant answered and she noticed how hostile her voice sounded:

"Antoine. He can't talk," she said in Creole.

I can't tell you how much I would have liked to ply Berthe with questions about that crucial moment!

"What did you feel?"

Feel? Feel? All the symptoms of passion when you have no idea of what passion is.

Let us try. Not to determine who was responsible — the heart is not responsible, the heart feels no guilt. Altagras was not guilty of idolizing her unfortunate son, an object of ridicule in their bourgeois world. Berthe was not guilty for feeling what she felt. Antoine was not guilty for inspiring and feeling so much love. Let's just try to understand. Up to then, Altagras had meant everything to her eldest son. She alone was able to make sense of the incoherent jabbering that would sometimes come from his lips; she alone could calm him down when he had his fits of rage, his "attacks," as the others said, in their mean objectivity; she alone could draw laughter from his taciturn mouth. Suddenly she had to share, and as we know, when you love, sharing is losing. She saw Antoine dogging someone else's footsteps like a shadow, waiting at the window for her return from school so he could jump on her excitedly like a puppy, then roll himself into a ball and stay in a corner of her room as she studiously did her homework, and finally pine away during the summer vacation when she was absent. A rival! And what kind of rival!

A little Negro girl with no father, whose mother was in a mental hospital, a girl she had taken into her home at her husband's insistence . . . !

From then on, two dreams shared Altagras's nights. We already know the first. Mano's Citroën hitting a palm tree on Dumanoir Drive, or his horse bolting and dragging him over trails full of volcanic rocks. The second: Berthe struck by one of those typhoid fevers that decimated Fort Pilote at the time, emptying herself of some putrid water through top and bottom. Or: Berthe bitten in the heel by a snake, a trigonocephalus, which likes to hide in the grass, and being found next to a bush, all swollen, purple, drooling from the lips.

Despite what was happening in her head and heart, Altagras remained an ardent Catholic, and so, the next morning, she would rush to church, lay bouquets of flowers at the feet of all the female saints, burn candles, and bury herself in a confessional. Father Van der Brucken would grant her absolution and lecture her:

"Come on, don't be too hard on yourself. Still, you can't wish for the death of a child, of a poor orphan you were good enough to take into your home. Besides, doesn't she make your son happy?"

Doesn't she make your son happy? That was exactly her crime!

As she came out of church, Altagras would meet shantytown children carrying the water their families needed for cooking and washing, for shantytowns were now starting to surround Fort Pilote. She would stop on the bridge over the Latania Tree River and watch the brown, foamy water, so cold at its source that you could chill soda bottles in it but gradually warming as it nears the sea. *   *

Historians tell us that those years were crucial for the country. According to what they say, the intrusion of industrial capitalism along with the mechanization of manual work brings about the breakup of traditional societies. Consequently, people here deserted the land and the urban centers grew. The population of Fort Pilote tripled and the shantytowns we have just mentioned sprang up. Likewise, our historians deplore the heavy drop in the sugar export business, which resulted in strikes by sugarcane cutters. They inform us of an increase in unemployment, illiteracy, and infant mortality. They talk of racial confrontations, and above all, they depict the "Bloody October Days" in great detail.

A relatively minor incident was at the root of those "days."

An old man nicknamed Magic Lantern made his living by putting steel tips on schoolchildren's shoes. To be more efficient, he had set up a kind of traveling stall outside the door of a very beautiful store called The Glass Slipper. He was an old Negro, honest and polite, but the problem was his presence on that piece of sidewalk: it didn't sit right with the owner of The Glass Slipper, a white man of Polish origin named Jaruzelski.

That man Jaruzelski would start calling him names over mere trifles. One day, whether it was because he hadn't screwed his wife very well or he'd caught her in bed with a lover, for she was a fast woman (to repeat what the gossips said), he was in such a terrible mood that he kicked the old man in the rear end and scattered his nails, pincers, leather patches, and steel tips all over the street. Two hours later The Glass Slipper was ransacked and Jaruzelski was pulled out from behind his counter and left for dead in the middle of the street.

All night long, a crowd crazed with anger set white people's cars on fire and vandalized their possessions. And things didn't stop at that. A construction worker, José Laran, stepped out of the background where he had remained till then. Standing on the balcony of the Chamber of Commerce, he exhorted the people to take their fate into their own hands, to drive out the whites and start a revolution as they had in some nearby islands. Students and intellectuals rallied around him. Of course, the disturbances were bloodily crushed by French forces sent over as a reinforcement. Handcuffed and in shackles, José Laran was put on a plane to answer to his crime before a special court of justice held in Versailles, former residence of the kings of France.

Such violence shows the extent of social tensions, but to those who might be surprised by this, we would say that as the economy collapsed, tourism was becoming the sole resource of the country. Europeans, mostly French, but also Canadians and Americans in search of sun and winter beaches and year-round casinos and night clubs, came flocking. White people all over. The well-known toleration threshold sociologists talk of had been reached, even exceeded. The natives no longer felt at home. Add to all that a new policy of transferring them to France . . . and it is easy to understand the reasons behind those spectacular reprisals. At any rate, this is what the analysts say in their writings.

What impression did these events leave in Berthe's mind? Practically none. The uproar of the great political struggles came to her muffled, from far away. From the "Bloody October Days" she remembered only a raging crowd pouring into the Rue du Sable. She watched it with Antoine and Dominique from the attic window and did not understand the reason for the angry cries and the signs they were carrying. After that, the Lycée Félix Eboué was shut down for a week. When it was reopened, she heard that some teachers had been transferred to France. Others had replaced them. Whites.

There is one memory, though, that stands out.

About the same time, six farmhands started a hunger strike in the Cathedral of Saint-Benoît to draw attention to their tragic situation. Growing sugarcane has always been a seasonal activity, from January through June, when it is harvested. After that, there is not much else to do: the cane does not require replanting since the same plants give a crop several years in a row. The workers in the sugar business are thus unemployed from August through December and have to live off their past wages.

As they were already wretchedly poor, they were condemned to a slow death when the monoculture export trade was abandoned. With Dorothée, one of her schoolmates, Berthe went to take a look at the men on strike who were lying on pallets in the transept of the cathedral. Even though she was born into the working class, she was not conscious of being a plebeian.

She felt no affinity between her and those Negroes with their emaciated faces and their frayed calico pants, short enough to show the yam-like bones right above their knotty feet; their women, wearing dark madras around their foreheads, would moisten the men's faces with water they drew out of calabashes. All these people smelled of sweat and poverty, odors she had never breathed before, and she ran back as fast as she could to the Rue du Sable, where a cup of hot chocolate and two slices of bread spread with guava jelly were waiting for her. For — and we must emphasize this — Altagras could never torment Berthe as she wanted to. As far as material things were concerned, the girl was always treated like all the other children in the family: Mano made sure she was.

If political events and the sight of the poverty her fellow citizens lived in left no impression on Berthe's mind, what then was able to move her, to stir something in her? It seems to have been the physical beauty of her country. Mano Aubrun had inherited from his father a house located in Raisins Clairs, a fishermen's village that had become a resort but had been spared the recent tourist boom. When, from a rocky peak overlooking the beach, Berthe saw the sea, the palm trees, the white sand, the delicate shape of a small island in the distance, she was convinced that in allotting her such a birthplace God had bestowed an immense privilege upon her. Likewise, every time she took the boat to go to Canete, once the pain of parting from Antoine had receded in her, she could not control an impulse to express her wonderment.

She would have liked to write poems. But who could she have showed them to? Antoine couldn't read.

I have hardly talked about Antoine so far, and to be honest, it is a real gap in the story.

A big boy, well built, like the hero Vitaliano Brancati tells us about in *Bel' Antonio*; when he came into the Cathedral of Saint-Benoît with his family, "the fairest eyes from the pulpit suddenly turned away." But not just to admire him, as they did during the first years of his life. It was to watch him dig his fingers into his nostrils, pull nervously on his curls, angrily roll his head on his mother's shoulder as if to get her to put an end to the torture she was subjecting him to. For if he was relatively manageable at home, Antoine was impossible in public. After he turned twelve, Altagras and Mano had to give up making him go out against his will. The house on the Rue du Sable opened onto a large garden where the cherrylike *quenette* and guava trees grew freely. Antoine spent most of his time there, half naked, lying in the sun, even in the afternoon sun that dries up all things, or tirelessly turning round and round on himself like a dervish.

Altagras would watch him from her bedroom window and breathe a silly prayer, her eyes filled with tears:

"Oh Lord, let him get well . . ."

All this stopped with Berthe's arrival, for thanks to her, he discovered painting. No one knows exactly how it happened. Probably, on a day when he was particularly demanding of her attention, she put brushes into his hands and encouraged him to smear paper with some paint. The fact is that this turned into a passion. When she was at school or doing her homework, he would untiringly paint vast frescoes whose tormented, poetic shapes came triumphantly straight from his imagination. Before long he started to paint the faces around him, and people were frightened to recognize themselves, similar yet different, undecipherable yet deciphered, secret yet uncovered. This became his way of communicating with those around him, especially with Altagras, for Berthe rarely appeared in his paintings (at least at the time; he started to paint her only after he had lost her). When he meant to show his love, Altagras appeared as a goddess or a siren with a hibiscus at the place of her navel and stars at her eyelids. When she had done something he did not like, she became the coarse trunk of a tree flanked by breasts hanging down like wineskins. He gave her two heads, three feet, a voluptuous mouth from which diamonds or toads fell at will, as in the fairy tale. In short, he possessed her as he pleased through his painting.

We must confess that at first, the family took Antoine's passion as something unimportant, an amusement for him. Mano, who was generous, open-handedly gave his poor son enough money to buy himself supplies at Prêcheur's, the only store for artists in Fort Pilote. Altagras actually had a number of paintings framed and had hung them here and there all over the house, not out of admiration but out of love for her son. Now, it turned out that one day, a friend who was returning from Haiti stopped short in front of one of these paintings and asked if it was not the work of a certain artist named Salnave Philippe Auguste.

To the amazement of the parents, he revealed the existence of Haitian folk painting, which the world's greatest museums were competing for, and of talented men who never had any schooling. He urged them to keep their eyes open, for they might very well be living with someone of immense talent. Altagras got very excited by the prospect but Mano kept cool. Pictorial art hadn't developed much in the country, although literature was flourishing. Mano himself had never opened a book written by one of his fellow citizens. Aimé Césaire's *Return to My Native Land*, which has been so influential, was unknown to him. All the great Russian novelists, from Tolstoy to Dostoyevsky, were present in his private library, but the only book of ours he had was *Fab'Compè Zicap*, Gilbert Gratiant's Creole stories; a luxurious edition of this work had been given to him as a present by one of his nephews but he had never read it. At the same time, he often complained about the mediocrity of the country's intellectual life. In ten years, he had never been to the theater and had seen only one film: an American adaptation of *War and Peace*. He had found it terribly disappointing.

5

I am now coming to one of the most difficult chapters of my story: the relationship between Berthe and Antoine. A difficult one, because neither of the protagonists ever confided to anyone about it. Antoine was obviously incapable of doing so; as for Berthe, even when cornered and harassed with questions, she never did. When did things change between them? At what point did they turn from a juvenile attachment — quite neurotic on Antoine's part — into a passion between a man and a woman with all its physical implications?

It is impossible to know. No one ever noticed anything. Not until Berthe's stomach started to swell, anyway. Swelling. The mountain of truth.

In that year, 1963, important events were taking place in Fort Pilote. For the first time, the words "independence" and "revolution" were no longer thrown into the air by a briefly overexcited mob and short-lived leaders; they were now being printed in manifestoes that expressed coherent programs, and they would soon be plastered on every wall in town on posters urging people to abstain in the elections. But Berthe did not care about all that. One morning at dawn, before the first mass, she was thrown out of the house on the Rue du Sable.

She apparently took refuge at the home of Destrella, a friend of Black-Eyed Martha who had known her as a little girl. This is where her son, Antoine, was born. Antoine, like his father. I have tried to reconstruct the nights Berthe had spent up to the birth of her child. From that time on, she started to think differently about Pourmera, her mother. I am absolutely sure of it. She could feel the scream Pourmera had given long before, a few weeks after giving birth to her, filling up her chest, creeping up slowly along her esophagus, through her throat and into her mouth, her lips opening up in spite of herself. She indeed carried the blood of that martyr, and she would soon meet the same fate. Be locked up between high walls. But madness picks its victims and Berthe did not seem attractive enough.

Antoine was born. A handsome child of 9 pounds and 5 ounces, and the nurses would gather by his crib to check if he really was the child of the Aubrun family's idiot son. Can you believe it, *chère*!

When Berthe took her son in her arms, she cried. She hadn't cried when she had met her mother, nor at the departure of Black-Eyed Martha and Marcius, nor when she had been thrown out of the house on the Rue du Sable and Antoine could do nothing to defend her. She cried. Not from sorrow but from love. She had wanted to die and here she was, giving life instead. She had thought she was all alone, abandoned, and now she had a companion. A weak one, and now her duty was to be strong. Strong for him.

The nursery school Achille-René Boisneuf has no memory of a child named Antoine Suréna who entered it in the very same year Fort Pilote was shaken by riots of unprecedented magnitude following the violent crackdown on the construction workers' strike. I was studying in Bordeaux at the time; terrified by the images of ransacking and destruction spread all over the newspapers, I spent my life on the phone.

"Don't worry," my mother kept saying. "They're only after the whites from France . . ."

That same year, our volcano we all thought asleep woke up, spitting up a thick mash of lava over a number of villages, and everybody thought our country had come to an end. An evacuation plan was put into action and the roads filled up with vehicles carrying children, mattresses, furniture. In the same year, Black-Eyed Martha and Marcius came back from Canete. Neither had any business skills, so not only had they dilapidated their relative's capital but they were head over ears in debt. They took Berthe and little Antoine back with them and the whole little crowd emigrated to Port Mahault, a pretty coastal town. Why Port Mahault? I'm not too sure . . . Did Black-Eyed Martha and Marcius ever act reproachful with Berthe? It's not very likely. She did after all give them the most beautiful present one can have. A child, a beautiful male child, brown and curly as a black–East-Indian mulatto, a *bata-kouli*.

For little Antoine, those years were years of complete happiness.

The road from Fort Pilote to Sofaya — the capital — runs along the sea going south. It first crosses a cane-growing area where the skeletons of shut-down factories now rise like so many ghosts, then it goes deep into the banana plantation region, scattered with poor-looking cabins half buried in the greenness. In order to get to Port Mahault, which is built on a sort of rocky neck of land thrust into the sea, you must leave the main road and go down a steep path near boulders engraved with strange figures, the work of the defunct Amerindians and the only thing those first inhabitants of the country left us.

Port Mahault brings together a small lighthouse, wooden cabins, concrete houses, a few grocery bars, a gas station, a covered market, a nice church, and a school not as out of proportion as it seems, when you think that it serves the children of hundreds of villages nestling in the twists and turns of the coast. A square shaded by flame trees and almond trees marks the center of town, and a walk lined with streetlights leads into a breakwater of dirty black stones. In Port Mahault, Marcius went back to his carpentry trade. But orders were scarce, so Black-Eyed Martha opened a *lolo* stall that sold a bit of everything: cooking oil, cinnamon, corned beef, sardines, needles and thread.

As for Berthe, she found a clerical job at the town hall in the office of the registry.

The moment he got out of school, Antoine would grab a fishing line and go after the small fish in the harbor with his friends. He never lacked change to buy sweets: "love pains" cookies and *douslets* or *sukakoko* candies. He was king in his family. The uncontested master.

In the early seventies, a man enters Berthe's life: Jean Larose, well known and appreciated in his community, for he was an excellent storyteller. I must confess he didn't seem to me a companion well suited for a young woman who, after all, had been raised in a middle-class family, had gone to a lycée for ten years, and had a job in the administration. But I may be influenced by my class prejudice. It's true that the Negro Jean Larose was no ordinary man: he was a skilled marine carpenter whose clients were the local fishermen; they ordered their boats from him — jolly boats, longboats, and dinghies. He turned out to be an extraordinary stepfather. When he left early at night to sail against the currents toward the ocean, changing tack frequently with his dinghy, he would set little Antoine at the bottom of the boat and put him in charge of preparing the lure. The child breathed in the night wind, his eyes following the crest of the waves and the swoops of the sea birds. At the same time, he would think of his mother, all curled up in the large bed he no longer shared with her.

For many years, Jean Larose gave Berthe and her son much happiness. Life is like that; it can grant moments of reprieve.

When did it all end?

There is record of a Company for Technical Assistance and Cooperation being established in Port Mahault to help fishermen get acquainted with the new technology, particularly with outboard motors. As a result, boat making was modified. The era of the traditional boat was over; Jean Larose lost his prestige and his orders.

That was when the people of Port Mahault remember seeing him staggering along the walk lined with street lamps and singing in Creole:

Doudou moin ka pati épi bom siro-la
Epi ki sa moin dousi kafé moin
Aie papa . . .

That is when he started beating Berthe. That is when people started to talk about little Antoine, who was not so little anymore but already quite big. The boy who used to bathe twice a day and rub his body with a handful of twisted leaves, his hair parted on the side and smoothed with brilliantine, was now neglecting himself; he was dirty and smelled of sweat. What had to happen did happen: at school, he dropped to last in his class. Marcius was struggling in his carpentry shop, so the idea of placing the boy with him as an apprentice came up. After all, there's no such thing as a stupid trade, and anything is better than hanging out on the street doing nothing. But Antoine looked his mother in the eye and said:

"I don't want to be a carpenter."

This calm impudence of his made Berthe fly off the handle. In a flash of memory, she relived all the sacrifices she had made, all the suffering she had gone through ever since she had opened her eyes onto the sun of this earth. She hit him. As hard as she could. Smack in the face. Antoine left without saying a word. I know what was going on in his life.

The year before, Mike Blustein, an art dealer well known all over the East Coast of the United States, was on his way back from Haiti, where he had ripped treasures away from starving people. He made a stop in Fort Pilote to have a taste of that Creole cuisine so highly vaunted in the travel brochures he had read: *The sophistication of France in a Caribbean setting.* By sheer chance, he happened to step into Prêcheur's, and there he pointed to a particular painting:

"Who did this ?"

"One of my cousins. He's a little . . ."

And the owner of Prêcheur's tapped his forehead in an eloquent gesture.

"Are there any other paintings? I want to see them."

He ended up calling the Rue du Sable. Altagras had been waiting for that phone call for over ten years.

What Mike Blustein saw there dazzled him: Salnave Philippe Auguste's sensitivity combined with the delicate and precise stroke of Philomé Obin, founder of the Ecole du Nord, and Hector Hyppolite's exuberance. As soon as he was back in New York, he set up an exhibit at the Parke Bennett Gallery and photographers came flocking to Fort Pilote to track down the artist. The French finally realized the existence of a genius in one of their possessions and a famous art magazine, *Connaissance des Arts*, devoted an article to him in its November 1976 issue.

Antoine Aubrun's masterwork is, in my opinion, the large painting entitled *Woman*. A figure in a red dress standing in a graveyard facing a purple sea, her oily skin lit by the glimmer of candles set up on the tombstones surrounding her. Some critics claim to see here the incarnation of the goddess Erzulie-Fréda-Dahomey, Agoué, the Great Bossine. They must be reminded that Antoine is not Haitian and probably never heard of the voodoo pantheon. As far as I'm concerned, the woman is Berthe.

What did Antoine know of his father at this point? Not much, I believe. He must have been told he was the son of a mulatto from a middle-class family who had abandoned him even before he was born. This is such common practice among us that perhaps he did not even think about it. But all of a sudden, his father's face was plastered on the front page of luxurious magazines from overseas. In one shot, Antoine was discovering that he was the son of a man who was an idiot as well as a genius; the two are not contradictory. Add to that the turmoil of puberty.

He took to running away from home. One of his escapades took him to Fort Pilote one day. He hung about the Rue du Sable. Every day at the end of the morning, under the scorching sun, Antoine Aubrun would leave home, for he could go out alone by then. Before crossing the street, he turned his head right, then left, his hands in the pockets of his calico pants. He would sit down on a bench on the Place de la Victoire and stare at the sea, concealed between the cars that had transformed a former paradise for encounters, innocent flirting, walks, and stolen kisses into a parking lot. Women wearing policemen's caps paced the walks, trying to avoid looking at the silent man always dressed in white who represented for them the martyrdom of a mother's heart.

It took a long time for the son to face his father. Hidden behind one of the venerable sandbox trees of the square, he was trying to find on that distorted face traces of his own, as yet unformed.

6

From 1978 on, I find Berthe back in Fort Pilote. She is living in one of those housing projects the communist administration has built on the outskirts of town; they spring up from the ground and surround the city with a concrete belt of cubes, with underpants, children's clothing, kitchen towels, and bed sheets flapping along their sides. She's had thoughts of leaving for France through the BUMIDOM, the office in charge of organizing the massive emigration of her fellow citizens for over ten years now. She dreams of becoming a nurse, thinking of her mother perhaps, now dead, who had been confined behind high walls for such a long time. Somebody convinces her not to leave, revealing to her that Paris is the cruelest city in the world; its celebrated beauty and feverish nights make the loneliness of someone without friends or family still harder to bear.

So Berthe is working at the Beautiful Books bookstore. She has the esteem of Monsieur Lucrétien, her boss. She never jibs at staying late evenings. She runs small errands for Madame Lucrétien. In exchange for so many favors, the eldest son of the Lucrétiens tutors Antoine in math. On Saturdays, especially in the period after summer vacations, Antoine helps out in the bookstore, which gives him a little cash.

A handsome boy, that Antoine. But he doesn't talk much,

he's touchy, stubborn. The teachers at the lycée complain about his sulky face. Yet, he is near the top of his class in French and history. I found a poem he wrote:

Our day will come — I am telling you
as true as the sun
as pure as beauty
as hard as metal
we will burn fascism
we will burn racism
and imperialism

A young rebel who doesn't quite know what name to give to his rebellion. Who uses words that don't exactly define his discomfort. For they are the only words that have been offered to him. There is a new man again in Berthe's life. He works as headwaiter at the Bananier, one of the hotels erected in the Goulet. His name is Edariste.

It's hard to realize that when I was a boy, the Goulet, located a few miles from Fort Pilote, was actually a small fishing town. The morning air was filled with the noise of the voices of men going fishing with their draw nets or trail nets. They were usually back at three. Some of them, who returned earlier than that, would go out again to haul up a few lobster traps, or pull into their casting nets some fish that would be used as bait for the next day's catch. The church bell called the women to the different masses of the day. But all of a sudden, as early as the sixties, world-class American-style hotels opened up one after the other. Between them, crafts boutiques, sadly presenting large *lambi* conch shells, stuffed swordfish, and Creole dolls for sale. It is so painful to watch your own country dying!

One year during the summer break from school, Antoine, upon the recommendation of his mother's lover, gets a job at the Bananier. It's hard to imagine him dressed in the absurd uniform of a waiter: white pants, red jacket sporting an embroidered emblem on its breast pocket, a madras tie. Actually, he doesn't last very long at this Bananier. They fire him at the end of the first three weeks. According to some reports, he allegedly was blamed for having instigated a strike among the lower-level employees: waiters, busboys, and chambermaids. This seems unlikely to me. I'm inclined to think there is some other reason. They may have asked him to trim his Afro, so he got angry and left.

At this time, two apparently unconnected events take place. Berthe becomes a Seventh Day Adventist and Antoine becomes the friend of Didier Réhat. Berthe had never been particularly attracted to religion before, and her conversion is rather surprising. What leads her to wrap a white kerchief around her forehead, give up eating pork, and sing with passion in a small tabernacle ablaze with heat? Perhaps because Edariste has left her to marry a Dominican woman. So she is tired of walking the path of life without a stick to lean on.

Still more surprising is the friendship between Antoine and Didier Réhat. Didier was the eldest son of Maximilien Réhat, the most hated man in the country. Ned, as his intimate circle and others called him, had made a smart move. As soon as the sugar industry started to decline, he quickly added his wife's land to his own and to the land of some neighbors who'd been ruined or expropriated with the government's blessing; in this way, he had acquired a thirty-thousand-acre property he had planted with bananas and had entrusted its management to a company of which he appointed himself CEO. He exploited his

farmworkers shamelessly. A great friend of the prefect and of
certain deputies, Ned ran the whole region. As is often the case
with boys of well-to-do families, it is easy to guess that Didier was
rebelling against his father. He probably thought that associating
with a half-black bastard who belonged to a social no man's
land was a smart, provocative kind of thing to do. But shouldn't
Antoine have been more suspicious? Apparently, he wasn't.

The two boys are inseparable. They go in tandem about Fort
Pilote's busy streets, among its garrulous crowd. They are the
same size, swap clothes, drink the same liquor, sleep with the
same girls. Well, no, actually the resemblance stops there. Didier
is the all-time great lover with a terrific line, making passes at
everything that wears a skirt. Antoine doesn't know how to
smile. The intensity of his eyes frightens people. He has a passion for Mauriac and reads his novel *The Little Misery* over and
over again. "Not now was it the King of the Alders who, in a
final gallop, was pursuing the boy, but the boy now who was
leading his uncrowned and insulted father toward the sleeping
waters of the weir, the pool in which the village boys bathed
naked. They were close now to the watery confines of that king-
dom . . ."

Often, at this point in his reading, he cries. So Didier makes
fun of him and hands him a glass of rum he does not drink.

In April 1981, a new political force, the ops, or Organization
for the People's Struggle, appears on the political scene. Its slo-
gans are no longer merely "Independence" and "Revolution,"
but "Armed Struggle" and "Urban Guerrilla." Living-room
speeches are now far away; every street corner is dripping with
blood. In front of churches, in the markets, on buses, that's all
people talk about.

Where will all this lead?

Personally, I admit I don't understand that rage and I'm scared. And yet, I can see how our country is being destroyed, I can see that we have no direct control, no power over the development of our society, that all the decisions come from somewhere else. I do know what we are suffering from. How well I understand the African poem:

Today man is no longer talking
he no longer holds the invisible salt between his fingers
nor shells the corn, he no longer carries ardent suns
or wears multicolored masks. Already the earth is forgetting his
    footprints . . .

But I'm only a doctor: my struggle is against disease and death. Soon, Didier and Antoine are flirting with the OPS. It is quite obvious that Antoine has acted under pressure from Didier. I have tried to delve into Antoine's personality by questioning his teachers and schoolmates. The same observation keeps coming back: "You could tell he was in pain." But no one ever bothered to find out where that pain came from.

Antoine never spent evenings at Didier's place, the Etranglée, a small house very tastefully restored by a California architect. As soon as the sun went down, he would rush upstairs to the fourth floor where his mother lived. The elevator no longer works: the good old firm of Roux and Combaluzier could not resist the assault of so many hands. The garbage chutes are clogged. A smell of sweet breadfruit, codfish, and fermented urine floats over the landings. Berthe is alone. She no longer yells at Antoine for the way he acts. She doesn't hit him anymore as she used to when he was a teenager. No; praying is enough for her now. A thick silence has settled between these two souls.

Berthe cooks the rice, washes and peels the tubers. Antoine does his homework in front of the white light of the television that rules the household, as it does the two thousand others in the project. As a matter of fact, he has only one thought in his head:

"Mother, tell me about him. Tell me how you fell in love. How you separated. Does he even know I exist?"

Altagras, who has become rich thanks to her son's genius, recognized at last, has donated one of Antoine's paintings to the new cultural center. It represents a woman. A woman once more, that's right! Her cheeks are blue. She holds a dagger in her left hand. An altar covered with blood, milk, and honey is set up before her. *Paris Match*, the big magazine from France, has just published a long story about the "Recluse of Fort Pilote." Berthe's son often plants himself in front of the fresco at the cultural center. He has cut out the photos from the story and keeps them hidden in one of his drawers. He doesn't know that his mother has noticed.

I have to say that like most people here in Fort Pilote, I don't much value Antoine Aubrun's paintings. In my opinion, they are mostly the scrawlings of a schizophrenic. I would like to be able to look at them at my leisure in order to extract a secret meaning from the network of lines and colors. But in truth, I'm not a good judge. I grew up admiring the great Impressionist masters: Cézanne, Van Gogh, Monet, Renoir, Pissarro, the Gauguin from before his *Vision after the Sermon*, a painting he made upon his return from Martinique. I remember how dazzled I was when I visited the Munich Pinakothek!

But I have no business talking about myself . . .

Antoine spends the 1981 summer vacation with Didier on the Ile aux Chèvres, a small islet north of our country. The Réhats own a country house out there. Once tobacco-growing land, nowadays the only resource of the Ile aux Chèvres is tourism because of the incredible beauty of its beaches. It is unthinkable for any tour targeting our country not to schedule a day on the Ile aux Chèvres. Thus, hotels have proliferated there, as well as those sad crafts boutiques. Not to mention the sailing crowd: the Americans, Canadians, and Scandinavians who come putting into its waters, sprinkling the sea with sailboats in some seasons.

I'm not too happy to see Antoine fly to the island with Didier, his sisters, his younger brothers, and his cousin Cyrille. I have a feeling some danger is on the way.

Without a care in the world, Antoine looks ecstatically at the landscape of the Ile aux Chèvres. Its main town, Fond Curé, reminds him of the Port Mahault of his childhood. Flowers everywhere: hibiscus, bougainvillea, *alamandas*, flowering lianas. Indian pear trees with knotty trunks line the streets. A graveyard with high black and white tombstones takes up the side of a bay and seems a proud city of the dead.

7

On 25 December 1981, as he was coming out of church right after midnight mass, which he had been attending with his whole family and his clan, Ned Réhat was murdered. Because of the international coverage it received at the time, this event is so widely known that I see no need to go into it.

I'm watching the funeral on television: Ned is treated the way the BBC would treat a member of the royal family. The storekeepers have shut their stores to protest the increase of violence, and in the dead streets, a huge crowd is following the hearse. To add more pomp to the ceremony, the family has restored the ancient custom of having the hearse drawn by animals, and four dappled gray horses draped in black move solemnly forward behind a brass band. The procession stops at every crossroad and the drummer beats his drum as if to warn whomever might not know it that death is passing by. Ned's widow, all dressed in black, is held up by her sons, among them Didier, whose face is drawn with grief. I would have liked this funeral to be attended by white people only. Far from it. The faces that flash by on the screen are of every color; they are the image of my country, where the darkest goes side by side with the lightest. There are men, women, children, old people. At the Briscaye cemetery, the priest gives a long homily. He prays that our wretched country may find peace again. Amazing! He exposes the injustice done to our farmers and farmworkers, the mad consumerism of the well-to-do classes that makes them forget their obligation of charity. Could it be that the Church is changing sides?

Of course, Ned's murder is a good pretext for banning the OPS, which from then on goes transparently underground.

More importantly—for my story at least—Antoine and Didier have stopped seeing one another. At school, they avoid each other.

There is a possible explanation. Ned's death has opened Didier's eyes. He has realized how much he loved his father and feels terrible about how he hurt him. So he is developing a feeling of guilt and is breaking with everything that reminds him of his rebellious past. I don't know why, but that explanation is not satisfying to me. It seems too simple, too obvious. There is something else.

After he had recovered from his adolescent crisis, Antoine had been one of the top students of his class; he drops to last again. He is often detained after school because he hasn't done his work. On Saturdays, you can see him at the Lycée Félix Eboué, throwing rocks at mangoes although it is forbidden by school rules.

Once, he is suspended for three days. He takes advantage of this to repaint his mother's place at the project and to put in nice, colorful tiles above the sink. Mother and son have reconnected. At night, they no longer watch stupid series on TV. They talk. About what?

About Antoine, of course. About the absent, mythical father.

"I never thought of him as being sick, mentally ill. He didn't talk, that's all. Aside from that, the expressions on his face meant more than so many superficial, ordinary words 'healthy' people use. I knew he had no power over his mother and I pictured him standing with his nose against the window, waiting for me to return. What had they told him to explain my absence? Oh, you have no idea how cruel that kind of family can be!'"

Actually, Antoine did have an idea, as I found out at last.

On 15 September 1981, Elodie Réhat was about to take Flight AF248 to Paris. She was flying business class and her whole family didn't let her out of their sight until she had passed the gate leading to the plane. Everyone agrees that Elodie was rather pretty. Her teachers were not impressed by her intelligence, with the exception of her English teacher, who was quite pleased with her: Elodie had an excellent accent. Of course she did, since she had attended Sarah Lawrence summer school in the States several times. An uncomplicated young woman, Ned's fourth child. In love with the idea of being in love and ready to fall for her brother's handsome friend. Considering the sexual freedom of our times, was there more than a simple flirtation between Antoine and Elodie? It doesn't really matter.

It is possible to paint Antoine as a young man scheming to introduce himself into a middle-class family and tarnish the honor of their virgin daughters in order to take revenge on the harm done to his mother and himself. That seems silly to me. A victim of the fascination the poor feel for the rich, he probably was sincerely in love. A mother with soft hands who has never scrubbed ragged clothes in her life. A father around the house, talking with his children about the books they read. (The international press emphasized the fact that Ned was a knowledgeable music lover, a great admirer of Mahler, who would cross the ocean to attend performances at the Met. Odd how torturers always seem to be such sensitive people! But let's not exaggerate;

Ned was no torturer. Just a capitalist.) With a swimming pool to rinse off the sea salt, lounge chairs by the pool to drink *maracuja* juice on the rocks, parasols as blue as the ocean, visible in the distance. Elodie was Antoine's farewell to the bourgeois world. His farewell to his illusions, to the confusions of his adolescence. He had read Marx and Engels, of course. He had even pinned on one of the walls in his room the famous passage: "The bourgeoisie has drowned the sacred thrills of religious ecstasy, of chivalric passion, of petty-bourgeois sentimentality in the chilly waters of selfish calculation. It has done away with the dignity of the individual, who has become a mere commodity." And yet, he did not understand. He could not understand that the bourgeoisie belongs to some other species. Despite his bravado and his inflammatory speeches, Didier had kicked him out like a dog when he dared to look at his sister. Exactly as his mother had been kicked out eighteen years earlier when she was pregnant with him. But now, Antoine knows. His looks change. No more Afro. No more of those fine dreadlocks. His head is shaved; so are his cheeks. He knows which way to go, straight in front of him like a furrow in a field. He strides through town and dreams of a better world, of a life that tastes of honey.

Oh, son I never had! If you had been mine, I would have guided your feet so they could find the flat stones in the ford.

Instead, you're getting badly scratched, you're bleeding!

A second independence organization appears; it is against the use of violence and for taking power through the legal process. As for Antoine, he gets actively involved in the ops.

For obvious reasons, I have been unable to pin down which actions he takes part in, or even whether he's actually a direct part of any action. Maybe he seemed too young, not reliable enough . . .

In June 1982, Antoine fails his *baccalauréat*. He announces to Berthe that he won't take the exam again. The mother cries: her dream had been to have a doctor for a son.

Antoine spends his summer vacation in Port Mahault. Black-Eyed Martha and Marcius are quite old by now. Marcius is suffering from a hernia, and the children have nicknamed him Banjo. He sits in the vegetable garden between the peppers and the water lemons and tells stories from the old days. He talks about the war, about Sorin the Vichy governor who wanted to keep the country under the bad Frenchmen. Antoine interrupts him:

"There is no such thing as two categories of French, the bad ones and the good ones. There are only colonizers. We must get rid of their control over us so we can build a classless, colorless society."

The old man gets angry. He wants to strike Antoine with his cane. The boy laughs, runs away, then comes back to plant a kiss on the forehead of the man he calls Grandpa.

Port Mahault has changed a great deal. No more fishermen mending nets with the wide brims of their straw hats down to their noses: nets are now made of nylon so they can't rot. Moreover, the technological revolution of the outboard motor has had the result of destocking the ocean depths. The men, who must now go farther and farther out to catch fish, get discouraged and turn away from the trade. They move to town and drive taxis. The day of the Assumption, 15 August, has been reduced to a tourist attraction. The only sign of authenticity is a reggae band from a nearby island.

They say that in the army
The girls are very fine . . .

Antoine sits at Pointe Curé and stares at the sea, a huge blue spot on the abused body of the earth. He has brought along a book he likes: J. S. Alexis's novel *Comrade General Sun*. But he doesn't read it. He stares at the sea. He would like to be a small child again, to go back into his mother's womb, swim in the sea of her womb. He is trying to relive the extraordinary affair between his mother and father. How did they say "I love you"? Where did they make love? In the attic during nap time. Altagras is thanking God: it didn't take Mano too long this time. She turns on her right side to deny his existence, fixes up her bun, throws herself on her pillow covered with an embroidered pillowcase now moist from sweat and cologne. She puts a perfumed handkerchief to her nose to cover up the smell of the man who has just mounted her. A few yards above her, on top of the three beams "bread-wine-poverty," Antoine and Berthe are wallowing in sex.

Night is falling. A hawk swoops down into the sea. Antoine goes back to town. In September he will start working as a gas attendant in that big, noisy gas station at the entrance to Fort Pilote. Painted like whores, the buses fill up there. They go all over the island and stop at the smallest places: Maringouin, Anse Mire, L'Etranglée, Fonds Cacao, Rivière Belle-Feuille. That year, a hurricane devastates our land. The wind creeps in through the disjointed wooden planks of the cabins. The sheets of tin roofing play flying saucers. The project houses leak at every seam. The banana trees kneel down, and from every chest, a cry wells out:

"Enough, O Lawd, enough!"

On 23 November 1982, the Paris daily *Le Monde* says:

"A hurricane named David has swept down upon some of the Caribbean islands, causing significant damage. There have been no casualties."

I look into Antoine's life for someone he might have loved. I can't find anyone. From time to time he spends a weekend with Leila, a pretty *chabine* who already has a six-year-old son named Gaël and works as a salesgirl at the Prisunic supermarket. The neighbors unanimously agree: he's very much involved with the child; he buys him "Ti Raccoon" T-shirts, calls him *ti mal*, "sonny," and teaches him how to box. But I happen to know that his heart is empty. There is room in it only for his mother. How he wants her old age to be a happy one! If only the taste of days could be different for her!

By the seaside, the coconut trees are lined up like the beads of a rosary. The year 1983 brings a string of terrorist attacks.

On 1 January 1984, Antoine buys tangerines for his mother so she can keep the pips and have a lot of money. He is on his way to meet his death and doesn't know it.

8

I may be blamed for having neglected Berthe. I do confess that youth has taken precedence over age, in my mind as well as in life.

Berthe has been in charge of the cash register at the Beautiful Books bookstore for years now. Every morning, before she settles into the glass cubicle that isolates her from the customers and the other employees, she has coffee with Madame Lucrétien. The coffee is as black as ink, as the blood of a bull. Both mothers are afraid for their sons; they sigh:

"They have their reasons."

Only once did Berthe have an impulse to oppose Antoine's "reasons" but she did it very clumsily. It was right after the explosion of the Emmelynck tower, which housed the independentist radio station. Four young men and women who had dreamed of a future without masters or servants, rich or poor, without white Creole *békés* or white French *métros* or Negroes or mulattoes, had been found buried under tons of cement, metal, glass, and plastic. Torn between terror and anger, Fort Pilote dreaded vengeance. Antoine had gone out, had come back, then gone out again after long, mysterious meetings outside the door while Yellowman was singing behind the cinderblock wall:

They say that in the army
The girls are very fine . . .

Berthe was lying on her bed, a bed Marcius had carved out of locust wood just for her, deep as a coffin. And her past was coming back to her in waves. Antoine — Was it the father or the son? In her love, she mixed them up — his hand slightly sticky in hers, while very dark, ragged kids sang about selling their magic for the price of two walnuts. Was she going to lose the son as surely as she had lost the father? The son turned up at six in the morning. Down in the yard, at the foot of the building, roosters were shaking themselves off in puddles of light. The sun, not yet cut at the neck, was starting to bawl. A surge of violence came over Berthe. She got up, all stiff in her flannel nightgown, and walked to Antoine's room. She feverishly piled against the door the dresser, the table, the guaiacum chest of drawers — an imitation Henry II — all remnants of her mother's possessions, ill at ease in that poor household, like a rich relative. Antoine was yelling, torn between laughter and exasperation:

"Mama, what are you doing?"

She left him locked up for two days. Two days with nothing to eat or drink. When she opened the door again, they fell into each other's arms. She was sobbing:

"D'you want, can I make you some *pisket* fish fritters?"

For weeks after that scene, the project apartment was like the Minnegrotte that Gottfried von Strassburg talks about. Mother serving son, son serving mother, both strongly united by very pure love. The mother-son couple forms the ideal model found in tantrism. The mother is a goddess, the cosmic female principle. There is no sexual intercourse. Everyone reaches happiness through the annihilation of the self.

Then things went back to the way they were before. Every morning at seven, Berthe rushes to the bookstore with her shopping bag. She first makes a stop at the Marché de Fer, the market not far from the Carrefour des Bossales. She bargains at length over Congo peas, small pink *christophine* peppers, over the *lambi* conch shells with their purple, sulfurous flesh. She trots about in her freshly pressed dress, patting the sapodilla cheek of a child here and there. Around eight, Antoine gets on his bicycle to go to his gas station. Despite himself, Yellowman's words are singing in his head:

Hey-hey, hey-hey, hey-hey
They say that in the army
The guns are very fine
I asked for an M16
They gave me an M9 . . .

Oh yes, he would love to grab that M16 and blow up the world . . . And then, from the ruins, build justice, joy, beauty. He takes part in every single action of the OPS. He works lovingly at making Molotov cocktails.

I'm through with my story, or rather, their story.

I'm not the best of witnesses. I am a mature man, sheltered in the selfishness of a bachelor's life. I'm putting an end to my family tree in the tall house on the Rue d'Ennery where we have lived since the beginning of the century. I never wanted to move out of the La Folie neighborhood, nor out of this house, unlike my fellow doctors who live farther and farther out in villas guarded by Cuban watchdogs. Too many memories keep me here. The memory of my mother first. I put on the piano the enlargement of the photo I took of her the last time I saw her, in Bordeaux. She's wearing a fur jacket. Fox, I think. Her hair is carefully straightened and waved out in stiff curls. But I have no business talking about myself when I should only be talking about them. About him mostly. Some saw his death as a punishment of the gods. Who lives by the sword shall die by the sword. And he who breaks his mother's heart, his seed will not bear fruit. Personally, I don't see him that way. He is a martyr for a cause that is bound to triumph someday. In the course of my patient quest to piece together these bits of scattered lives, I interviewed nearly two hundred witnesses. I will only quote M. Hippolite, the owner of the gas station where Antoine worked. He shrugged his shoulders:

"What can I tell you? He was a kid like any other . . ."

Nanna-ya

For Cheryl and Michael Pash

1

How strange that twenty years after her mother returned to the earth whose color she was, Grace cannot spend a single day without thinking about her. And yet, when she was alive, she had hardly loved her. Feared her, instead.

First, because of her physical appearance, which was unusual even for this region where women were as vigorous as men. Since her conversion, she always wore a black, shapeless dress as if she wanted to hide the generous forms of her figure from everyone. But Jane could tame a rebellious horse one-handed and take him back to his corral with his nostrils foaming. She could also shake the coconuts off a coconut tree and then split them with one blow of her machete. Grace had feared her because of what people used to say about her, too. The story went that before her conversion and her baptism a few miles up, in Berridale, in the waters of the Rio Grande that cut like crystal, Jane had the powers of an obeah, a healer. She knew how to communicate with spirits and could cure anything. One day, they brought her a little boy all torn up by a bull's horn and left for dead. Closing her eyes, she had laid her hands on the horrible wound, and the ripped flesh had closed over. As for the boy, he had slipped into a deep sleep and when he woke up couldn't remember a thing. Grace had never been to a doctor once in all her childhood. Every morning at dawn, Jane dragged her, still heavy with sleep, under the porch roof made of three sheets of corrugated iron; turning her toward the rising sun, muttering an incomprehensible litany, she bathed her in a decoction of leaves and roots and then put a pinch of powder tasting of sea salt on her tongue.

Jane didn't talk much about herself. In Moore Town, everybody knew that her family had the legendary Nanny, the war horse, as a direct ancestor. After the great battle of 1734, the destruction of Nanny Town by the British garrison, and the signing of the peace treaty with the British, Kwesi, one of the sons of the indomitable fighter, had settled in Moore Town while the others fled west. Kwesi's descendants did nothing that recalled their origins. Over the years, little by little, nothing set them apart from the rest of the maroons anymore; warriors turned farmers, they lived frugally off the products of the land and raised pigs that paddled around in the mud of the gullies along with the children. But in Moore Town, Cornwall Barracks, and all the way to Comfort Castle on the other side of the river, they continued to be regarded with special respect, and people still credited them with unique powers.

When Jane's stomach started to swell unmistakably, everyone held their breath in amazement. She was known to be uncompromising. The year before, with one whack of her hand, she had sent John Harris, one of the colonel's sons, rolling in the dust because he had dared to say something to her about the beauty of her eyes. So everybody wondered about the man who had succeeded in laying her down on her back and inflicting such a wound on her. Yet the prestige of Nanny's offspring was so great that no one would have risked a joke or even a smile about it. That astonishing pregnancy was almost looked upon as the mysterious work of some ancestor who had turned into a god and had the idea of lifting up his fallen people. Neither Jane's father nor her numerous brothers, uncles, and cousins would walk into Ginger Tavern with their heads down when they came in to play craps. Jane herself carried her belly with pride.

Every Wednesday, she would take the family plantains, manioc, yams, and avocados down to the Port Antonio market and walk back up before nightfall with a handful of coins in a knotted handkerchief tucked between her magnificent breasts. Things changed a few weeks before the date the baby was due.

On one of those Wednesdays, it was well past ten and she was not back from Port Antonio yet. The whole neighborhood was alerted and joined the family to be on the lookout for her on the narrow road full of deep ruts that wound along the mountainside.

Around eleven, she suddenly appeared out of the night, recognizable by her huge stature yet completely different, staggering like a drunken man with her arms flailing. A wail was coming out of her lips, and as she reached the crossroad where one path goes up to fork off toward Berridale while the other drops suddenly toward Moore Town, she crashed down full length in the mud. Twenty hands, twenty arms reached out to pick her up, carry her to her father's house, and lay her down on her mother's bed. Then the door was shut. Her father escorted the neighbors up to the bamboo bridge that spanned the gully to thank them for their help, and once again, the night became prey only for fire beasts, stray dogs, and the spirits of the ancestors.

From that Wednesday on, Jane was not to be seen. Five weeks later, she gave birth to a girl.

People who live in Moore Town, Cornwall Barracks, and

Comfort Castle consider themselves as members of one big family because they all share the same ancestors: the maroons, those fearsome Africans who refused to be slaves on the plantations and took to the mountains. Whatever hurts one member hurts them all. When rumor had it that Jane's child was as white as the moon, the same shame, the same pain was felt under every single roof. How awful! The Koromantyn ancestors were surely turning over in their graves! As for fearless Nanny, had she fought to the death just so a white man could plant a child out of wedlock in her descendant's womb?

For the father was probably one of those uncouth, rakish American sailors who came to Port Antonio aboard the United Fruit Company banana boats. Others claimed it must have been some Englishman, a planter or a merchant or a servant of His Majesty, for many of them lived in that part of the country, playing cricket or polo under the envious eyes of ragged little Negro boys. Soon, a new rumor swept away all these suppositions. It became known that Jane had converted and was to be baptized on a Sunday in the Rio Grande. Although missionaries of all denominations were very active in the region, their influence remained limited in Moore Town; during services, the audience was rather sparse in the pews of St. Peter, the small stone chapel, sad and silent as a grave among the graves of the churchyard. Jane had probably chosen the Baptist Church because of its abolitionist past but also because they tolerated the songs and dances that the Anglican Church considered pagan. The whole community came to Berridale to watch her enter the water with a dozen other novices dressed in white, holding palm branches in their hands and singing. Her strong voice rose above all the others. She had arranged white magnolia flowers in her hair. Never before did she look more like a pagan divinity as at the moment she was entrusting her life to the Christian God. From then on, she was never seen otherwise than dressed in black with a dull handkerchief wrapped around her forehead; she came and went, silent as a shadow. Her father gave her a small piece of land at the far limits of Fellowship. With her brothers' help, she built herself a little house, two rooms and a porch, in which to raise her daughter, Grace.

And Grace grew up hating Moore Town.

She hated the cirque of mountains that held her in a trap she would never be able to escape. To the right and left, summits draped in fog, blending into the gray color of the sky. As far as the eye could see, dense, hostile vegetation, always eager to devour the precarious gardens of man. Far away, the distant rumor of an unruly river that claimed its quota of victims every winter. But above all, she hated that maroon spirit, that maroon pride.

Nanna ya, nanna ya
Obu Oke Omo
Nanna ya, nanna ya . . .

The singsong of the children at school. That story was not hers, she knew it. Somewhere along the line, and just for her, the family tree had broken and a shoot of unknown origin had appeared. Her golden skin and her long braided hair swinging on her shoulders were a constant reminder of it. No one in the Moore Town family or in the nearby communities ever made the slightest remark to her, mocked her, or hurt her with sharp words. It seemed, instead, that she had a privileged spot in everyone's heart.

Her grandmother Maddah Louise particularly adored her.

Maddah Louise was a maroon from Seaman's Valley and it was said of her that like all the people in the area, some of the blood of the Englishman George Fuller ran in her veins. Not as dark, not as statuesque as her children, as her daughter Jane especially. She started to learn to read and write so she could be a guide to her granddaughter, and soon she could be heard reading slowly and hesitantly along with the child or singing silly songs with her. On Sundays, when she got out of church, deafened by the din of the handbells and tambourines, terrified by the shouts and gesticulations of the people the Spirit possessed before it had them lying down, all broken and sweaty at the foot of the altar, Grace would lay her head on the old bosom. Maddah Louise would take little pieces of smoked pork she kept warm on a fire of green wood and slip them between the girl's lips, then make her drink a mixture of honey and liquorice water in little gulps. Unfortunately, Maddah Louise died when Grace was seven, and with her, all sweetness vanished from her life.

Grace interrupted her task for a while and mopped her brow. It was hot, very hot for December, usually a humid, rainy month.

Yes, not a day went by when she didn't think about her mother. A mother she had not loved. Feared, instead. Or more precisely, a mother she had started to love only after she died, like a fallen tree whose foliage you begin to miss. When she was alive, Jane was too big, too formidable. You could neither look her in the eye nor kiss her mouth. You could only disappear into her shadow.

Jane saved every penny so Grace could study at the University of Kingston. For times had changed. The bananas from the Portland region were afflicted with the mysterious Panama disease, and the United Fruit Company was turning away from them to stretch its tentacles out toward Mexico, Venezuela, or Columbia. Port Antonio attracted only American eccentrics by now, as on the other side of the mountains, Kingston, the town hastily built to shelter the survivors of the Port Royal earthquake, had claimed the rank of capital and was becoming a commercial and intellectual center. But Grace cared little about going to Kingston and climbing, one by one, the endless steps of secondary, then university, education. Her only dream was to get away as quickly as possible. Fate took the shape of Gloria Pereira, a charming young girl whose family was from Port Maria and who became her best friend at the Sisters' school. Gloria invited her to her birthday party. As Grace muttered some terrified excuses, Gloria went up to Moore Town with her mother to sway Jane; she succeeded without too much trouble. Gloria had a half-brother, George Jr., who helped his father with the books in the hardware store he had just bought back from Wong, the Chinese. In the course of the party, he smiled at Grace. She smiled eagerly back and three months later they were married. Grace remembered the talk she had with her mother. It was morning. All night long, she had summoned up her courage. Jane was standing under the porch roof of the kitchen and was drinking one of those herb teas only she knew how to make. Her face was turned to the east and the sun was diffidently brushing her inflexible features. Grace stepped forward and delivered her speech all in one breath. Jane put down her little *coui*, half a hollowed gourd, on the table, turned to her daughter, and said simply:

"This is not the kind of life I dreamed of for you . . ."
Grace found somewhere in herself the strength to reply:
"This the life *I* want . . ."
Jane didn't seem to hear and went on:

"They built a university in Kingston. Soon the whites will leave the country and things will be like they were before . . ."

Grace shrugged her shoulders as a feeling of pity mixed with anger came over her:

"It won't be like before! Never again. There's no point in fighting the whites or avoiding them anymore. We must learn to live with them, and worse still, live like them . . ."

Once again, Jane didn't seem to have heard:

"And the whole country will belong only to its children . . ."

Grace nearly laughed, but she controlled herself and repeated:

"This is the kind of life *I* want . . ."

Three months later, she got married. Six months later, Jane was gone.

One Friday morning, a small cousin came down to Moore Town on a donkey, his back, black as slate, showing through his ragged shirt. He informed Grace that her mother "was not well."

"What's wrong with her?"

The child made a gesture of ignorance. The following Sunday after mass, Grace and George Jr. went up to Moore Town. Jane was dead. She had already been washed, perfumed, and dressed in a long white gown by the women of the family. Half the people of Moore Town, Cornwall Barracks, and Comfort Castle were crowding into the two rooms of the little house. The other half stood on the porch or in the nearby vegetable garden. This whole crowd stared at Grace accusingly. Those stares have haunted her ever since. She poured the cane juice spiced with lemon peel into the cup, put the two hot patties on the saucer, and held out the tray to Sonia, the young servant who had been staring at her all along, transfixed by the minute precision of her gestures:

"Take this to Master."

George Pereira looked at his watch: ten o'clock. At that exact moment, there was a knock on the door and Sonia came in with the tray of light snacks. Once again, if he'd wanted to catch his wife out, he was stopped in his tracks.

George Pereira Jr. was born in Coleraine, a banana and sugar-cane plantation his mother worked on. She had died a few hours after giving birth to him, but under pressure from the priest bending over her bedside, she had agreed to whisper the name of the father. Unwilling to waste the time it would have taken to close her eyes and calm the cries of the other women, he wrapped the newborn baby in a piece of towel and rode his donkey to Port Maria, where Neville Pereira lived.

Neville Pereira was a crossbreed of Indian, Chinese, and white. He said he owed his name to some Spanish ancestor who had traveled to the area to sell Cuban watchdogs to the British so he could help them bring down the maroons. He had fallen in love with the region, settled in, and founded a family.

He was a rich merchant, but he never made a show of his money. A God-fearing and honest man, he sang the psalms louder than everybody else at mass on Sundays. He had seven sons, three from a first marriage with a Negro woman from Oracabassa and four by a Scotswoman, a minister's daughter, and so he could say with a big, hearty laugh that he had worked for racial harmony.

When the priest presented himself at Neville Pereira's house, the family was sitting at the dinner table. As soon as he saw him,

George, the third son, who had just turned eighteen, got up abruptly, made a move as if to rush to his room, then sat down again and laid his head on the table, sobbing, thus giving clear proofs of his guilt. Neville Pereira looked at him in silence, then turned to the priest:

"What is it?"

"A boy . . ."

"The mother?"

"Dead . . ."

The newborn baby was named George, like his father. At the Pereiras, George Jr. was never subjected to any injustice or abused in any way. But you can't prevent a child from probing people's hearts and feeling his difference; and it hurts. After all, he was a mere bastard and the darkest in the whole family to boot. His grandfather was the only one who didn't seem to notice at all. To make up for this, little George invented a new family tree for himself. On his deceased mother's side, the peasant from Coleraine, he descended from Tacky, the famous slave who in 1760 had been the leader of one of the greatest uprisings in the area. George went into ecstasies over what had actually been a guerrilla war and cost the lives of over three hundred men on both sides. To please the child, Neville, whose imagination was quite fertile, embellished the meager information provided by the chronicle of the local historians. He even started to take him to the very place where the uprising had originated. Actually, there was nothing left of Frontier Plantation or the slave cabins bordering the cane fields. Nature had reclaimed these places. Fig trees spread out their branches, which met the eternal, majestic foliage of the trees of life. George dreamed, trying to imagine the actions that had occurred two centuries earlier: Negroes crouching under giant ferns with fear in their guts and love of freedom in their hearts. Then George would see his grandfather holding his beautiful horse by the bridle while he grazed. The past was gone. What would his life be like?

Around 1950, George Pereira, who was over thirty, dared to take a stand against his father, claiming that Bustamante was a great man. Right there and then, Neville scrupulously handed over to him the portion of inheritance to which he was entitled and threw him out of the house. George, who adored his brothers, could not go very far. He settled a little farther east on the coast, in Port Antonio, with the young woman he had just married. There, he bought back his store from Wong, the Chinese, and spurred by his father's example, was not long in becoming a rich man. George Jr., who was twelve at the time, never got over that separation from his grandfather. His temperament, already somewhat uncommunicative, became even gloomier. Soon he fell to last in his class, so his father, whose business kept growing and who needed help, took him into the store, where he taught him bookkeeping.

As he was nearing his sixteenth birthday, his grandfather died. Neville was a strong man who had never seen a doctor and treated himself with plants according to recipes he had learned from his first wife. One evening, he contracted a high fever. He snapped at his wife, who wanted to give him quinine, drank some decoction of his own composition, and went to bed. He passed away during the night. The next morning, his wife, who had been sleeping in another room so as not to disturb him, found him all stiff, already exuding a sickly-sweet smell.

For George Jr. it was a terrible shock.

The worst was that Neville had given away his personal belongings to his family and friends, in writing: his pocket watch, his Scottish pipes, his Bible, his leather-bound collection of narratives of voyages of discovery. But he had left nothing to his grandson. No matter how often he was told that death had caught Neville by surprise, leaving him no time to update his list of gifts, George Jr. felt abandoned, betrayed.

As soon as he had asked Grace to marry him, George had the feeling he was trapped. The very day after his wedding night, he started looking for reasons to resent his wife. She was fragile, shy, quiet. Then his hatred found a precise object. Wasn't she a descendant of the maroons? After the agreement signed with the English, wasn't it a maroon that had aimed at Tacky with his long contraband gun and killed him with a shot to the head? Tacky, his hero, possibly his ancestor!

From then on, he had but one ambition. He was going to write a "History of Tacky"; not only would it be an homage to a martyr, but at the same time it would illustrate the sad story of the maroons, those freedom fighters paradoxically turned watchdogs for the English whenever someone else's freedom was at stake. He ordered a Remington typewriter from Kingston, reams of strong and onionskin paper, and started his work.

George Jr. had taken over his father's store, hardly modernizing it, while his three brothers were off first to Kingston, then to England or the United States. His sister, Grace's former girlfriend, had married a man from Trinidad and had left to live in Sangre Grande. On the rare occasions when there was a family reunion, George felt like an outsider. His brothers would talk about politics, a topic he hated because Neville Pereira had told him a thousand times that politicians were vile creatures who put themselves above God and claimed the right to destroy His laws. The independence of his country, proclaimed when he was around twenty, had meant nothing to him. He was just starting to recover from his grandfather's death at the time. The right to vote, which his people gained in 1944 at such a heavy price, was something he never used himself, for the ballot box, with its obscene slit, symbolized a terrible sin in his eyes, just as bad as the sin of the flesh. In Port Antonio, he watched the arrival of the tourists' seasonal migration: English and Americans on their way to Berridale, where they would take rafts to go down to the mouth of the Rio Grande. But then all that activity had stopped for a while. He had heard that the country was going through a socialist phase and consequently there was confusion and violence everywhere. Then, the migration had resumed.

Now George often thought of himself as some sort of fossil, a laminaria hooked to its rock and tirelessly washed by the sea. So he would take refuge in his "History of Tacky." He forced himself to work at it three hours a day on weekdays, all of Saturday, and all Sunday when he came back from church. As he progressed in his work, new horizons opened up before him. He wanted to paint the life of the eighteenth-century planters, the relationship between Britain and the rest of the world, the origin of the slaves, and above all, the relationship between the maroons and the slave population living in the plains. It was to be the centerpiece of the book. Oh, how much he wanted to destroy the myth that had formed around them. His manuscript was almost one thousand pages long and far from being completed. But time meant little for a work of such magnitude!

Recently, though, a new element had entered George's life: love (but was it love?) for another woman, a child almost.

Some men are meant for adultery and take it in their stride. George did not belong to that category and agonized over it. He wished his wife would free him of his pain and leave him, as she was well aware of everything. But it was not like her to act that way. She stayed there, irreproachable, obedient as a bitch in its kennel. One day, he dared to open up to Father Charles, the one who had wrapped him in a piece of towel at his birth, thus pulling him out of a future of poverty. The old man had shrugged his shoulders:

"What is it you are blaming your wife for? Everybody envies you . . ."

George had said in a whisper:

"Father, I love elsewhere . . ."

The priest's only answer had been to open his Bible and ask his interlocutor to join him in prayer.

George finished eating his patties, wiped his mouth, and called Sonia, who was waiting in the store, chatting and laughing with the two salesmen. She came in, suddenly putting on her face a mask of deep respect, and George, moved by the absurd desire to see her smile and become animated, slipped his hand into his pocket:

"Here, this is for you . . ."

Her stupefaction hurt him. Yes, in everybody's eyes, he passed for a stingy, self-centered man with no redeeming qualities. And it was all his wife's fault! If he hadn't rushed into this stupid marriage at the age of twenty-two, he would have been a completely different man. But he was going to amaze them all with his "History of Tacky" . . .

A few years earlier, a minister of the government had come to inaugurate a monument to Tacky, built next to the Presbyterian church in Port Maria. George had made the trip for the occasion, taking with him Frank, his favorite son, the spitting image of his revered grandfather. All along the ride, he had talked to him about Tacky, what he meant to him, about the history he was writing, of his pride in seeing that he was finally recognized as almost a national hero. And then, just when the minister, in his alpaca suit, bare-headed under the sun, was cutting the symbolic ribbon, the child had started to cry. As George, gently but firmly, was ordering him to be quiet, he had started to howl through a fit of sobs:

"Mommy, I want my mommy . . ."

His own children did not belong to him. He was unable to communicate with them. What impassable screen was separating them? George pushed away his accounting book, put his hands on his desk, and remained there, motionless, staring at a spot of light.

Joyce half opened the door and smiled. Then she shook her head:

"The reading room is closed, Michael."

The child frowned and asked:

"Why, Miss . . . ?"

"I have to go meet someone very important who came all the way from Kingston just to see me . . . and Lucy didn't come to work this morning. Come back around one-thirty. I'll be back for sure."

Without saying a word, he turned away, walked to his bicycle, got on it, and disappeared. Joyce locked the door and came back to examine herself in the mirror. She liked what she saw. She couldn't help being coquettish, even in that small town, lost at the foot of the mountains, encompassed by the sea. To be sure, she had a special reason to look good on that particular morning.

Joyce was the daughter of a Jamaican sailor who had settled in Folkestone in England between the two wars and married the barmaid of the bar where he got drunk every night. She had never bothered to learn why her father had become an expatriate and had grown up in that town, constantly changing from a place swept by spindrifts to a lively resort. A town she had thought was her own. She was intelligent and had graduated from secretarial school without much effort. She was looking for an office job when once, joking with a regular like herself in a pub she had been going to for years, she suddenly heard him say to her rather harshly:

"Listen, Topsy! If you don't like it here, go back home . . ."

Home?

She remained petrified. Home? Was it Jamaica then, that faraway island her father talked about only with his drinking buddies? Never with his children. Less even with his wife. As if it were a topic forbidden to intruders. She took up the challenge. She learned then that Jamaica had become an independent country in 1962, a few years after she was born, that it was a tourist's paradise, that Noel Coward had fallen in love with it and settled on a headland rising over the sea. All this meant little to her, so she had borrowed a hundred pounds from her brother who sold insurance and bought a plane ticket. Three months later, she found herself head librarian in Port Antonio.

Port Antonio can be called a pretty town. It is one of the few towns in Jamaica where Georgian-style buildings going back to the time of King George III still remain relatively intact: the Court House and some of the houses on High Street. The Anglican church has its charm too, tucked between clumps of royal palm trees, a bit incongruous here against the gray, mossy stone. But mostly, it is the moving purple belt of the sea that gives it beauty. As life is very quiet here in Port Antonio, Joyce thought at first she would die of boredom. No pubs where you could play darts while eating sausages. No discos where you could listen to the Beatles. Only one theater where they showed karate

films. But little by little, she got a feel for the place. And moreover, her life, which would have remained anonymous if she
had stayed in Folkestone, became a soap opera with episodes
written by some inventive writer as it went along. The color of
her skin — the reason she had fled England — paradoxically put
her in a superior social class from the start. All the people
employed in service jobs or working in the lowest positions or
toiling in the fields were black. Like her father. All of a sudden,
she understood why he had fled. As for those with light skin
like herself, they could dare anything if they played their cards
right. At the same time, her position as a librarian, humble
under other skies, conferred intellectual prestige on her here.
From plain Joyce, Marjorie's girl, she had risen to Miss Campbell, someone who almost had real social status.

The Port Antonio public library, located inside an ultramod-
ern concrete rectangular building, was composed of two large
rooms, a reading room for children and a reading room for
adults; and in between, a smaller circular room decorated with
travel posters liberally given out by the agencies, where periodi-
cals were displayed. When Joyce arrived, her predecessor had
resigned; she had given up, tired of material obstacles and general indifference. She, on the other hand, settled down to her
task with great enthusiasm. She quickly understood that she had
to direct her efforts at the children — little boys, and little girls
with bows in their hair, who took possession of the streets twice
a day at the exact same time. So she went to visit the Sisters and
the principals of the nonreligious schools, and in less than a
year, she had tripled the numbers of readers under the age of
fifteen. But as for the adult section, she had to admit her lack
of success. She only had a half-dozen members. Among them,
George Pereira. He had come in one afternoon, a short while

before closing time. He was very tall, built like an athlete, undeniably handsome, yet awkward, ill at ease. He had explained:

"The librarian before you used to order certain kinds of books from Kingston for me."

"What kinds of books?"

He got flustered and she wouldn't have been surprised to hear him mumble:

"Pornography . . ."

Instead, he said:

"History books. I'm doing research on a slave uprising that happened here in this area in the eighteenth century. It's very hard because slaves are the invisible agents of history . . ."

She repeated, involuntarily mocking him:

"The agents of history despite themselves . . . ?"

He got still more flustered, if possible:

"I mean, if you study the planter class, it's very easy. There are plenty of documents: large houses, portraits, writings, but for the slaves, there is nothing . . . just your imagination . . ."

And he had started talking about Tacky . . .

Coming from someone else, such babbling would have bored her to death and she would have stopped it. But something in that secretly wounded, vulnerable man reminded her of her father. Why hadn't she ever bothered to get to know him more? So she offered George a chair and pretended to hang on his every word.

Joyce lived right in the center of Port Antonio in a boarding house that sheltered few permanent guests but served lunch to a number of impecunious tourists and hurried travelers. From then on, every evening at nine, George came to see her there. He would walk across the unkept garden where bougainvilleas, Indian almond trees, and tulip trees grew freely, greet the owner,

Mrs. Boyd, who lived on the first floor, and rush up the staircase. What kind of excuses did he make up to free himself for the evening? Joyce avoided the question. What where the stages, the groping, the confidences, the declarations of love that had led them to that point in their relationship? She could hardly remember. At first, his subtle resemblance to her father had moved her. By showing interest in him, she nurtured the illusion of righting a very old wrong. When she tried to back off, it was too late. And for almost three years now, she had been angered by her truncated nights and all that mess encrusted in her youth, which was so promising in all other ways.

A few months earlier, on a whim, she had insisted on spending a week with him at Montego Bay. One week — seven full nights, that is.

George was a rich man who didn't know how to handle money. He had no use for credit cards and didn't trust checks. When he learned that hotels on the North Coast wanted to be paid in foreign currency, he went through a process of exchanging money at the Central Bank when it would have been so much simpler and quicker to go through the black market that everybody else dealt in openly. Finally, he obtained a fat stack of green bills, all alike in his eyes, that he carefully examined under the ironic looks of the waiters. On those idyllic beaches, so different from the beaches in Folkestone or Dover, the sight of all the white, half-naked bodies exposed to the sun and the sea only stirred in him images of vice and perversion. While he was there fulminating, Joyce would shrug and repeat:

"They're only tourists, just tourists . . ."

One evening, she dragged him to the Bangarang. The Bangarang was not one of those sterilized, air-conditioned nightclubs for tourists, where the wildest rhythms would be Harry Belafonte's calypsos. It was a hot, burning cave. There, in a deafening blast of decibels, men and women worshiped sex the way only God should be worshiped. While she was wiggling her hips on the dance floor with a boy of her own age, he disappeared. She met him back at the hotel. In other words, all day long, he was both pathetic and irritating, like a distraught minister, shocked by the vulgarity and thirst for pleasure of a society eager to make up for four centuries of colonization.

Only at night was he bearable. Then, he would be Master again.

It was at Montego Bay that she made the decision to leave Port Antonio and break up with George. He was only a dead weight in her life. Yes, if she made the right moves, the world, this world, would be hers. A bit of intelligence, a bit of dynamism, a lot of ambition, would do the trick. This society, like a female, was awaiting the enterprising male who would know how to conquer her! How different from England where everyone plodded in a furrow traced in advance.

Turning her back on the Court House, Joyce went up High Street to the bus terminal with its street vendors selling chicken and smoked pork, passed John's music store, bellowing out reggae as it did every day, and arrived in front of the board of education building. She knew the place, for she had often haunted it in her quest for funds and book donations, so she went straight up to the first secretary's office. He was not alone but in the company of a well-dressed, rather young-looking man, evidently a city man. The stranger smiled, his eyes expressing his surprise at seeing such a charming and modern person in such a place, and he stepped forward:

"My name is Richard Scott. I'm one of the associate directors of the Jamaican Institute."

2

When her husband's affair with Joyce had started, Grace knew that it was the culmination of her mother's vengeance. What offering could she make to calm her angry spirit? Milk, fruit, and blood of the goat, arranged in a *coui* with a handful of flowers? In the past, Jane used to place such offerings next to the graves scattered over the mountainside. She would kneel down by each of them and whisper some mysterious words. Then she would get up, fix her black, shapeless dress, pull her handkerchief over her forehead, and walk back home. Grace would follow her, splashing for fun in the puddles of the path. Why hadn't she paid more attention to the words and gestures of her mother? As she didn't know what else she could do, she had lost herself in prayer, but with the feeling that the cold services of George's Anglican Church would never allow her to restore that broken communication. To rekindle the dead fire. To restore the warmth.

Yes, Jane was taking revenge for not having been loved. Feared, instead. For having faced death all alone.

One day, Grace had gone up to visit her uncle Tim, her mother's youngest brother. It was the time of the banana harvest. Small boys in rags were pushing heavy wagons in front of them, loaded with big bunches of bananas lying on beds of dried leaves;

later, the fruit would be found on the tables of Europe. Trucks were waiting at crossroads out there. Tim had come in from the fields with his hoe and machete in his hands, and Grace hadn't been able to say anything. How could she bring it up?

"Tell me about her. About her last moments. Did she ask for me? Death wears a black muslin scarf. She wraps her victims in it . . ."

Grace got settled in the large conjugal bed and took *Animal Farm* from the bedside table. With George at Joyce's place and the children watching television at the neighbors', she filled the long hours she spent alone each evening by reading the books her oldest son sent her from Toronto along with a short note explaining difficult or slightly risqué passages. Little by little, a kind of fatalism had taken her over, and she had grown to enjoy this solitude, this peace. As it was close to nine, she expected George, who was working in his office, to come into the bedroom, grab the keys of the old Buick he had bought secondhand the year before, and disappear without saying a word. Instead, he came out of the bathroom in his wrinkled pajamas with the top half open on his massive chest where his hair was starting to turn gray. She was so surprised that she nearly pointed out what time it was, almost asked a question, but then restrained herself. As he paid no attention to her presence, she went back to her reading. After a while, he took the book out of her hands, skimmed through it randomly with a sarcastic expression on his face, then handed it back to her, still without a word and with the same pout. Then he lay down on the bed. Suddenly, he turned off her bedside lamp:

"Do you want to prevent me from sleeping, is that the idea?"

A few years after they had been married, as he was making love to her, George had stopped and asked Grace:

"You don't like it, do you?"

She had answered under her breath:

"You're the one who doesn't love me . . ."

It had been their only moment of truth.

In the course of their twenty years together, aside from the weeks when Grace slept with her newborn child in a small room at the far end of the gallery, the couple had always shared the bedroom, and there had hardly been a night when George didn't possess the passive and at the same time recalcitrant body of his wife. She never refused him, for she did not consider that embrace as a humiliating act or as the ultimate aggression; she welcomed it instead as an admission of his weakness.

That night, George made love to Grace with all the rage of his wounded pride. Joyce had called him at four to tell him she wouldn't be able to see him because she was having dinner with some friends at the Hotel Bellevue. Who were those friends? Where were they from? As he was pressuring her with questions, she had hung up on him. So he had closed his books, stepped into the store where Sam and Ben were exchanging stupid jokes, and with just one look reduced them to silence. Then, he had crossed the street to order Victor to turn down the volume of his damn boom box. At least if he played harmonious tunes! But no, of course not! They were reggaes, a cacophony invented by the most dangerous of sects. To George, Rastafarianism was an abominable heresy. Turning a small emperor who had been deposed by his people and died ignominiously into God, into the Creator! When he moved away from Grace, though, he felt better, and something almost like gratitude came over him. So he made a proposal:

"What would you say if we took a trip?"

Grace wasn't sure she had heard right and she repeated:

"A trip? Did you say a trip?"

George grew impatient:

"I did say a trip . . ."

"What would I do with the children?"

"Can't you ask someone from Moore Town to come down here for a while?"

Grace was dumbfounded, as George hated her family, and she repeated:

"A trip? Where? Why?"

The only trip she would have liked to take was the trip from Port Antonio to Toronto to hug her boy. George sat up straight on his pillows:

"I have to go to Kingston to meet with the representative of a British publisher whose address I got from someone. It's for my work on Tacky . . ."

After twenty years of hearing about that "History of Tacky," Grace, and the children too for that matter, didn't believe it would ever be finished or published. Besides, she had no desire to see it happen, since the whole thing was essentially an engine of war, partly directed against her, intended to destroy the little she had of familial pride. She said, skeptically:

"You finished it?"

"A few months ago, I wrote the words THE END, the most beautiful words in the language. Then, I gave the manuscript to be typed."

"To whom?"

George got flustered:

"To a reliable person . . ."

Guessing who that "reliable person" was, Grace dared to murmur:

"Why didn't you send the manuscript for John to take care of? It would be safer . . ."

George turned his back on her:

"I never took my sons for my masters . . ."

Then he didn't say another word. For Grace's remark had awakened a fear he was carrying deep inside him. Ever since he had entrusted Joyce with his life's work — twelve hundred scribbled, scratched-out pages — she kept saying she was making progress with the typing, but she hadn't produced a single page yet. Knowing how irritable and impertinent she was, he didn't dare ask her about it. But he was in agony. Had she lost the precious document that would at last make him a man above all men? The people of Port Antonio, everybody who had belittled him, would gather in awe. So, a genius was hiding in their ranks and they had mistaken him for a merchant, an importer of pots and electric fans? George lived his life over again. All those needle stings that had made him the suffering, bleeding soul he now was.

Once, when he was a boy, he had been playing in front of his grandfather's door and a fat woman had walked straight up to him and called out sharply:

"Hey, your mom works here? Go ask her if they need another maid . . ."

As a teenager, he used to help his father in the store, so he would go to the train station or to the customs office, where the employees would treat him with a familiarity he hated:

"You go tell your bloody boss . . ."

His brothers would explain behind his back:

"We don't have the same mother . . . his mother was . . ."

That's why, in his father's living room, which had been scrubbed since morning with a handful of leaves so the wood could retain its scented, tart smell, he had smiled at Grace. She was the only approachable girl in that flower-bed circle of arrogant little mulattas in their three-flounced taffeta dresses and high-heeled shoes; they all would have ordered him to "keep his paws off" as if to a dog. The only approachable girl. But once involved with her, he had realized how pathetic his catch was. A bastard like himself, straight out of the belly of an illiterate Negro woman, who was supposed to be an obeah and who spoke the rough Creole of the mountains. Unfortunately, it was too late to back out, and he had been forced to live his life with that fake piece of junk jewelry.

George attempted to ease the very old pain that was coming over him, but a new pain was now adding to it. Where was Joyce? What was she doing? He was like a condemned man who knows his days are numbered but doesn't know how his end will come. Where was the little bitch?

At that moment, Richard Scott was looking at Joyce, feeling extremely distrustful. All those affected looks, all those smiles! He was dealing with a coquette and a schemer. And then, his intelligence found it suspicious that such a young woman, a newcomer to the area, could have put together a compilation of this kind. What were her sources? Who did she get her information from? The whole thing posed serious historiographical problems. But this high-yellow girl was so gorgeous, with her very curly, blond hair and her green eyes speckled with gold! Richard Scott loved women. Aside from that weakness, he was a very serious man. A historian, a professor at the university, and an associate director of the Jamaican Institute, he had made a name for himself through a remarkable study of the uprising led by Sam Sharpe — one of the national heroes. Under the previous regime, he had been cultural attaché in Cuba, and even now, when the Jamaican Embassy in Cuba was closed, he saw to it that some exchanges were maintained between the two countries ... He had come to inform Joyce that she was the winner of the Norman Manley Prize for history, but actually, without seeming to, he wanted to grill her from different angles. Yet there he was, letting himself be dragged into an affair he didn't really want. He tried to collect himself and said coldly:

"How were you able to collect such impressive documentation on Tacky? I mean, Nanny, Sam Sharpe, Paul Bogle ... are all much better known. Look at my work for instance, or Braithwaite's work, or even what Sylvia Winter, V. S. Reid, and Orlando Patterson have done in the field of literature ... And what about you? How did you proceed? Where did you start from?"

Joyce didn't bat an eyelid:

"I was lucky enough to get to know someone who said he was a descendent of Tacky's. In reality, he didn't have a clue. It was purely a figment of his imagination."

Richard Scott laughed:

"That may well be the only real heredity! The imagination!"

When Joyce had met George, she had hardly paid any attention to his talk about writing the "History of Tacky." To her, it was just innocuous babbling. A whim. One day, he had brought her twelve hundred handwritten pages and she had skimmed through them out of curiosity. Unreadable. She had thrown them into a drawer. The way she could take advantage of the manuscript had only become clear to her when she opened the *Daily Gleaner*. There was an announcement for a national competition for the Norman Manley Prize in three fields: poetry, fiction, and history. The Norman Manley Prize was not as prestigious as the Casa de las Americas Prize but it was just as important, for attached to it was a scholarship or professional promotion, as the case might be. So Joyce had gone back to the shapeless narrative, terribly written, solemn and pompous as the sermon of a minister preaching in the pulpit, interrupted with digressions, idle considerations about the country and the times, and sententious discourses. Ah, but there was as much of George as there was of herself in the story she had sent to the Jamaican Institute! She had cut. She had rewritten. She was the one who had thought of using the first person:

You have asked me to tell you the reasons that prompted me to undertake this account of the insurrection, as you call it. To me, however, it was a struggle for freedom and dignity. Thus I must go back to the time of my early childhood, even to the times before my birth. I turned 31 on October 2 and I was born on Frontier Plantation, in St. Mary's parish. There was an event in my childhood that left an indelible impression on my mind. It became the basis of the enthusiasm that led so many black and white people to such a fatal end. It has to be told here. As trifling as it may seem, this event is at the root of this belief of mine, which has never left me and has grown stronger with time. When I was three or four years old, as I was playing with other children, I happened to tell them about some uprising that had taken place before my birth in that very same district of St. Mary's; there was no way I could have known about it since my mother had never told me about that uprising. I nevertheless stuck to my story and related some facts that tended to confirm it. Other people were called in and were greatly moved. They knew that the rebellion had actually taken place and had been bloodily crushed so that our people might never lose the fear of engaging in that kind of action. So it was said of me that I would surely become a prophet since the Lord had showed me things which had happened before my coming into the world. But my way of explaining it was completely different. I was convinced that my destiny was to lead my people to freedom . . .

"That person you are talking about, the one who gave you all this information, where is he?"

Joyce came back to earth. She had anticipated everything:

"In Folkestone. He was a friend of my father's. He used to tell us the story of Tacky evening after evening. We didn't take him seriously, but when I arrived in this area, I saw the monument in Port Maria and I realized that there was some truth in all this. So I started to go hunting. Our people have a fantastic memory, you know . . ."

As she said that, she had such a charming way of smiling that she dissipated Richard Scott's last scruples. He said softly:

"How about going dancing somewhere?"

She smiled again, mockingly this time:

"In Port Antonio, it's kind of hard . . ."

"Well, let's go to Ocho Rios then . . . It won't take long by car."

He waved to the waiter.

Richard was Joyce's only chance to leave without delay, without waiting for the news to be spread over the front page of the *Daily Gleaner*. She had to put miles between her and George. Yet she was not afraid. She would stand before any court to defend herself. No panel would have accepted and awarded a prize to the brew George had concocted if she hadn't put her own seasoning in it. At the same time, she knew he wouldn't put up a fight. He would be fatalistic about the whole thing, take it as another twist of his constantly hostile fate.

Richard Scott got up, a little hesitant but already defenseless, the victim of something instinctive, stronger than his reason. All of a sudden, he remembered that he had promised Trevor Howard, whose struggle he admired even though he didn't entirely share his views, to attend his rallies in Berridale. Too late! He could spend the weekend with Joyce in Ocho Rios; then they would leisurely drive down to Kingston . . .

3

Old Chang's store had known better days. Twenty years back, aside from Wong, Chang had been the only shopkeeper in town; he sold everything they needed to the people of Port Antonio and its surroundings — without ever giving them credit. It went from salt to corned beef to lard, including of course, all the local produce peasants brought him on the backs of their donkeys: plantains, green bananas, sweet potatoes. Then, times had changed. With more money in their pockets, people had become harder to please: they wanted goods like eggs, bacon, rice, vegetables. Finally, independence had confirmed the rise of an active, bustling middle class connected by invisible threads to London, Toronto, Miami. Most of the Chinese had adjusted to this new clientele. The Wong brothers, for instance, had founded a chain of supermarkets, and you could find their stores in every town of the country. Old Chang had not yielded to that trend, and little by little, his customers had deserted him. In his smoky shop that seemed to have blackened, cans of food were stacked on the shelves and two huge candy jars sat on the counter. By the door, an old Roberval scale allowed him to weigh the supplies a few faithful farmers still brought him.

For the last twenty years, Chang had been the sole news agent for the *Daily Gleaner*, and in that respect at least, aside from the kids who sold it on the streets, no one competed with him. Old Chang opened the newspaper as he did every morning. A NEW LOAN FROM THE IMF. He shook his head and went quickly to the next page. A country that lives on loans is like a shopkeeper who can't balance his books. Doomed to bankruptcy. RACE RIOTS IN MIAMI. And the niggers keep flocking there! Why don't they kill them all! He turned the page again. BLACK MARKET IN DOLLARS: HOW TO END IT? Old Chang laughed openly at this. That'll be the day! On page 4, the picture of a familiar face. With the caption: "Joyce Campbell, winner of the Norman Manley Prize for her 'History of Tacky.'" Dumfounded, Old Chang took his pipe out of his mouth. He remained silent for a few minutes, then regained the use of speech and called his wife:

"Shawn!"

Shawn appeared, holding her daughter's latest baby in her arms.

Like Shawn's, Old Chang's ancestors were driven out of California by anti-Chinese riots and settled in Port Antonio in 1870; they had never married the Negroes or the colored people around them, but that hadn't prevented them from forging strong friendships with their neighbors. Old Chang had seen George Jr. in khaki shorts in his father's store, and from time to time, he had downed a glass of Appleton with father and son. In his emotion, he called out:

"Come here, come here!"

Shawn obeyed him and leaned over the page of the newspaper her husband handed her. Joyce's disappearance had caused quite a stir already. Overnight, Lucy, her assistant, had found herself all alone in the library and was at a loss to answer the questions people kept assaulting her with. The wise ones would shake their heads:

"There has to be a man behind this . . ."

So they kept coming back to that man from Kingston, who some said had offered her a position. A position? What kind of position? Why? And who was that man?

Now at last, everything was becoming clear.

For George Pereira's passionate interest in Tacky was no secret in Port Antonio. It was almost part of the collective unconscious, just as certain historical facts were: the emancipation of the slaves, the Morant Bay rebellion, the death of Bustamante, for instance . . . Of course nobody really believed he was doing research. People knew he thought about it and that was enough.

Shawn said softly:

"Men are so crazy! Why did he give her his work?"

Chang nearly choked:

"What do you mean, give! He didn't give her anything. She stole it from him and that's why she ran away . . ."

It didn't take long for all of Port Antonio to reach the same conclusions as Old Chang. People who never bought the *Daily Gleaner* because they found it too dumb and too pro-government snatched it out of each other's hands in order to read the incredible news with their very own eyes: Joyce Campbell had scrammed and she was getting the Norman Manley Prize with a story she'd stolen from her former lover. There were mothers to claim that they never trusted her, forgetting how much her golden skin had made them wish she could be their daughter-in-law. Some, very few, felt sorry for George. The general feeling was that he was getting a fair punishment for his arrogance, for having humiliated his wife too much, and because he'd had a good time with a girl everyone else wanted.

Grace called in her last-born, Yvonne, who was playing in the yard and said:
"Come and eat, I made pancakes . . ."
The child, trying to assert her budding personality, replied:
"But I don't want any pancakes!"
Grace took her in her arms and begged:
"Give me a kiss . . ."
Taken aback, for her mother didn't show tenderness openly, she obeyed her. The fact is Grace was suffering. George was so changed ever since Joyce had left that she couldn't recognize him anymore. She had learned to live with his stubborn silences, his hidden bitterness, his contempt. But now he seemed inhabited by a great calm, indifferent to everything beside himself. In waiting. And she would have liked to shake him by the shoulders and say:
"Wake up. She'll never come back. Ever."
She put Yvonne down, then sat her in front of the table.
At that moment, Sonia knocked at the back door, came in, and put down that morning's shopping bags. Grace took the *Daily Gleaner* from her hands and mechanically leafed through it.
"Joyce Campbell was born in Folkestone. She illustrates the vitality of Jamaican immigration which has proved itself in so many fields, especially in music. She arrived three years ago in the province of Portland and developed a passionate interest in the figure of one of our heroes and martyrs, the rebel slave Tacky . . ."
Her first reaction was one of incredulity. Why on earth did

George give her his manuscript? Then the truth dawned on her. So that's why she had run away! She got up, walked over to the window, staring at the oblong fruits and cracked trunk of a *jacquier* without seeing them. It had poured all night long. The backyard smelled of mud, steam, and green leaves that had warmed up in the sun. Was this her mother's hand?

By removing the source of her pain, Jane was giving back to her a man who could only hate her more. For he would obviously need some kind of nutriment to fill the emptiness of his life, to nurse his hurt and humiliation. Twice betrayed. Twice forsaken. Sex and mind. Cruel mother, pretending to take pity on her child when she was really mocking her!

Grace came back to the center of the room. Her hands performed a succession of mechanical actions, and finally they placed the *Daily Gleaner* on George's breakfast tray, which she handed to Sonia:

"Take this to Master . . ."

The servant started up the staircase. She had been working for the Pereiras for four years now and only once had they given her a raise. She couldn't go on like this. But every time she made an attempt to bring the matter up, Grace would find some excuse. Sonia had no respect for these women, reduced to zombies in their own homes. Her mother had raised five children without a man around. Her eldest sister was doing the same. So she was all set to go to George himself. Personally, as far as she was concerned, she wasn't scared of him. When she walked into the room, she saw him curled up on the bed, his face turned to the window, which was already framing a bright rectangle. She put the tray down and resolutely said:

"Mister George . . ."

He turned to her in such a tired way, gazed at her with such sad eyes set deep in their orbits, that she took pity on him. She said softly:

"Mister George, are you sick?"

Without saying anything, he rumpled the sheet between his hands, like a dying man, and she repeated:

"Are you sick?"

He shook his head and raised himself up on his pillows.

Night comes down so fast over Port Antonio! If only it could linger a little longer over the twin bays before weighing on the serrated leaves of the breadfruit tree and the funereal flowers of the frangipanes! It would rain again tonight. The clouds were getting ready to burst above the John Crow mountains, whose peaks were partly disappearing into the dark. Port Antonio was living its brief nocturnal life. Spangles of light flashing at the windows. Sophisticated voices from the television, talking about shores that would never be reached. Cries of children. Neon lights of the stores ... Grace resigned herself to opening the bedroom door.

All day long, she had put a succession of actions between her and that familiar gesture. The last one was reading the story of Winnie the Pooh to Yvonne, who knew it by heart and could recite whole sentences before her mother did. After she had fallen asleep, Grace tiptoed out.

George was sitting on the bed; near him, the tray with his dinner left untouched, and in front of him, the *Daily Gleaner* opened to the fateful page. Over the course of their many years together, Grace had never seen him like this. When he was sick — a bout of fever during the rainy season — he would go to the garden, pick some leaves from the lemon tree, the soursop tree, some wild mint and lemongrass, flavor them with cinnamon bark and thousands of other plants, and prepare some kind of herb tea for himself made according to his grandfather's recipes. After lovemaking, Grace would never dare touch his back again, arrogant, already hostile. For the first time now, she saw him armorless, naked, bleeding. She sat down on the bed, took his hand, and he didn't shrink back. He didn't reject her. She dared another gesture and he fell on her chest, gasping uncontrollably. Could it be her mother's hand, after all?

She thought she knew what he felt. Like a woman who gives birth to a stillborn child after an unbearably long pregnancy. So many hopes, so many plans that would never come through. Communication broken off. Never will I look deep into your eyes. Never will I get a smile from you. My Lord, have mercy!

He stammered:

"But why? Why?"

She stroked his rough hair. Her tenderness, her love, carried inside her for so long, surged from her belly to her heart to her lips and overwhelmed her, preventing her from saying anything at first. Then she managed to whisper:

"It's better this way, George. That story of Tacky, you were using it to cause pain. To me. To others. And in the end, you were hurting yourself as well. But now . . . Now . . ."